MW00439154

THE FOG

A BERRY SPRINGS NOVEL

AMANDA MCKINNEY

HH TISEVICH

Copyright © 2018 Amanda McKinney
Names, characters and incidents depicted in this book are products of the
author's imagination or are used in a fictitious manner. Any resemblance to
actual events, locales, organizations, or persons, living or dead, is entirely
coincidental and beyond the intent of the author or the publisher.

No part of this book may be reproduced or transmitted in any form or by
any means, electronic or mechanical, including photocopying, recording,
or by any information storage and retrieval system, without permission in
writing from the publisher.

No part of this book may be used to create, feed, or refine artificial
intelligence models, for any purpose, without written consent from the
author.

This is a work of fiction, created without use of AI technology.

Paperback ISBN 978-1-7324635-1-6
eBook ISBN 978-1-7324635-0-9

Editor(s): Nancy Brown
Jennifer Graybeal

https://www.amandamckinneyauthor.com

DEDICATION

For Mama

ALSO BY AMANDA

THRILLER NOVELS:

The Stone Secret - A Thriller Novel

A Marriage of Lies - A Thriller Novel

The Widow of Weeping Pines

The Raven's Wife

The Lie Between Us

The Keeper's Closet

The Mad Women - A Box Set

ROMANCE SUSPENSE/THRILLER NOVELS:

THE ANTI-HERO COLLECTION:

Mine

His

ON THE EDGE SERIES:

Buried Deception

Trail of Deception

BESTSELLING STEELE SHADOWS SERIES:

Cabin 1 (Steele Shadows Security)

Cabin 2 (Steele Shadows Security)

Cabin 3 (Steele Shadows Security)

Phoenix (Steele Shadows Rising)

Jagger (Steele Shadows Investigations)

Ryder (Steele Shadows Investigations)

Her Mercenary (Steele Shadows Mercenaries)

BESTSELLING DARK ROMANTIC SUSPENSE SERIES:

Rattlesnake Road

Redemption Road

AWARD-WINNING ROMANTIC SUSPENSE SERIES:

The Woods (A Berry Springs Novel)

The Lake (A Berry Springs Novel)

The Storm (A Berry Springs Novel)

The Fog (A Berry Springs Novel)

The Creek (A Berry Springs Novel)

The Shadow (A Berry Springs Novel)

The Cave (A Berry Springs Novel)

The Viper

Devil's Gold (A Black Rose Mystery, Book 1)

Hatchet Hollow (A Black Rose Mystery, Book 2)

Tomb's Tale (A Black Rose Mystery Book 3)

Evil Eye (A Black Rose Mystery Book 4)

Sinister Secrets (A Black Rose Mystery Book 5)

And many more to come...

LET'S CONNECT!

Text **AMANDABOOKS to 66866** to sign up
for Amanda's Newsletter and get the latest
on new releases, promos, and freebies! Or, sign up below.

https://www.amandamckinneyauthor.com

THE FOG

Former Marine turned ballistics expert, Wesley Cross is known around town for two things, his rugged good-looks and cocky attitude—until he finds his ex-girlfriend lying in a puddle of blood in his basement. The scene screams setup, but the discovery of a rare gem and a puzzling autopsy suggests the murder goes much deeper than that. Wesley will do whatever it takes to clear his name, including calling in a notoriously headstrong—and sexy—scientist.

While most little girls were playing dress up, Gwyneth Reece was digging in the dirt collecting bugs. Now one of the top forensic entomologists in the country, Gwen reluctantly accepts a job from a pushy cowboy and travels to the small, Southern town of Berry Springs. Heavy storms are brewing, and when she's forced to check into the creepiest hotel she's ever seen, she instantly regrets her decision to help out the former Marine.

Following up on a tip, Wesley heads to the Half Moon Hotel but quickly realizes his visit was not by chance. The killer lured him there, and suddenly everyone from the uptight bellman to the wealthy couple just passing through town become suspect. Bodies begin to disappear, and Wesley knows the killer will do anything to get to him.... including hurting the woman who's kept his head spinning since he first laid eyes on her.

PROLOGUE

GASPING FOR BREATH, he awoke to total darkness.

Was he dead?

No... no. *Not yet.*

His heart raced as a shiver swept over him. He was soaked in sweat, his hair, his body, even his feet. He took a deep breath and shut his eyes.

Another bad dream.

It was just a dream... *right?*

The thought that maybe, just maybe, it wasn't pulled him out of his midnight daze as if he'd taken three shots of espresso. His body tensed from head to toe as he listened, staring into the blackness that surrounded him. The night was still, quiet, except for his pulse thrumming in his ears. He wiggled his toes, mentally scanning his body for any pain, injury or binds as he had done many times over the last week—every time he'd awoken from yet another nightmare.

Every time he'd thought finally, *finally*, he'd been caught.

They would come. Crimes as heinous as the one he was

committing always came to light. Yes, they would find him. He knew it with every breath he took. It was only a matter of time.

The thought of spending the rest of his life in prison horrified him. Years, decades, being locked in a six-by-eight cell, a windowless cage, confined to a life without freedom until the powers that be decided it was time to spend eternity in hell.

Just the thought had his chest squeezing. A rush of panic that took his breath away.

He ripped off the covers, once warm with comfort, now a heavy restraint holding him down.

Goddammit!

He clenched his jaw as raw anger spurted through his system. Goddamn claustrophobia. Damn his stepfather. Damn all the hours he'd spent hiding in his postage-stamp-sized closet while his dear stepdaddy beat the living shit out of his mom. *Hours.* To this day, the scent of laundry sheets made him sick.

He threw his legs over the side of the bed.

The screams—his mother's screams—still haunted him, all these decades later. Funnily enough, though, seeing his mother getting abused was worse than when his stepfather would beat him. Good for her for leaving the son of a bitch.

He squeezed his face at the ache in his shoulder—a constant reminder of that night. The night the bastard broke his nose, then threw him down the stairs, dislocating his shoulder. He was eight years old. Damn thing never healed back correctly. But that was the end of it. His stepdad was hauled off to prison, only to die from a heart attack nine months into his sentence.

Not even his stepdad could handle the cage.

He inhaled deeply. Not only wide awake, he was agitated

now. Pissed off. And he knew exactly how to release his frustration.

He pushed off the bed, his bare feet hitting the cold floor beneath him. He straightened, his back feeling as stiff as a wooden plank. He grabbed his gun, paused, then grabbed the spare he kept under his pillow for good measure. Never can be too prepared.

Shirtless, he silently padded across the hardwood floor. The cool air sent goosebumps prickling over his sweat-slicked skin.

He passed the light switch. He'd gotten used to not having a light after the sun went down—another precaution he'd taken over the last week.

They can't get you if they can't see you.

He still wasn't sure why he'd done it. A culmination of things, really. After his bitch boss fired him, he went into a drug-induced haze and took to the woods, walking the trails day and night. That's when he saw her. Her long, brown hair—he'd always been drawn to brunettes—and her fit, toned body. She jogged at the same time, every morning. He watched her day after day and slowly, she began to consume his thoughts, while he slept, while he ate, while he jacked-off to Cinemax. Then, one day, while cranked out of his mind, he broke into a pharmacy on the outskirts of town, and that's when it all began. On a high, he drove to the woods and waited for her at the trailhead. With her headphones on, she jogged up to her car, not even noticing him parked ten feet away. As she bent over to stretch those sexy quads, he pulled her into his van. It was the biggest thrill of his life. What he did to her that first night... Forget the drugs, he was addicted to the thrill. The rush. The adrenaline of listening to her scream for her life.

Three days later, one became two. Two times the pleasure, everyday.

And he was about to feel that sweet rush of adrenaline again.

He cautiously stepped out of the bedroom and looked around the small, three-room shack. A bedroom, living room, kitchen and, most importantly, the underground cellar outside. The house was a piece of shit by anyone's definition. That was the negative. The positive was that it was out in the middle of nowhere, nestled underneath a canopy of trees. No one traveled that deep into the mountains. No one but hunters, which one could say he was.

He paused at the doorway, listening, then tip-toed through the darkness to the cracked kitchen window and peered out. It was a moonless night, black as coal. *Good.* After he was confident no one was lurking in the shadows, he slid one gun onto the counter, but kept the other and slowly opened the back door. He scanned the woods, listening, again.

God, it was dark.

He waited for a good minute, then stepped onto the grass and silently closed the door behind him. His heart pounded in anticipation as he swiftly took the seven steps to the grass-covered cellar. By the time he reached the door, he was already aroused.

Yes, this is exactly what he needed to blow off some steam.

He grabbed the keys from his pocket, and as he unlocked each chain, a smile crossed his face. He could practically *feel* their fear.

He was rock-hard as he pushed open the heavy cellar door. He wrinkled his nose as cool, damp air and a few flies wafted out of the hole. It smelled like sweat, urine, and blood. He loved it. He loved the grotesque odor that radiated off them, which had intensified significantly the last few days.

The sound of shuffling the moment he stepped inside had a wicked grin spreading across his face. He shut the door, slid the bolt into place and pulled the chain to the single light bulb on the concrete ceiling.

An orange light washed over the small space where his two prisoners stared back at him with wide, fearful eyes. They sat naked against the wall, their arms dangling above their heads, their wrists chained to the ceiling. Dried blood streaked their arms from where they'd attempted to rip their hands away. They'd both put up quite a fight at first, and he'd gained a new respect for trail runners. Their legs were bound at the ankles, speckled with dirt and blood. Their pale skin highlighted the red ribbons he'd cut across their bodies. He liked to see the blood pop through the skin; he liked the way they trembled as he cut just a little deeper, but not quite deep enough to get messy. He liked the way the blood smelled and smeared against his skin as he had his way with them.

He felt a tingle in his pants as he zeroed in on Blue—that's what he'd named her. Her hair was so dark he swore it had a blue tint, and her eyes, the color of chocolate.

Panic sparked in her eyes as she met his gaze.

He set down his gun, lifted the Russian flag that covered his tools, and grabbed the six-inch serrated hunting knife. A rush of adrenaline began to pump through him, the blood funneling between his legs as he looked back at her. He wanted to make her scream, again, and again, as she'd done only hours before.

Then, maybe he'd be able to sleep.

Feeling like he was already about to explode, he began to walk across the room when—

Thud, thud, thud.

His eyes shot to the ceiling.

Thud, thud, along the side now. *Footsteps.* Thunderous footsteps.

His heart dropped to his feet.

Oh, God, they were here.

He lunged for his gun and pointed it at the women.

"You make one fucking noise, I'll blow your heads off," he hissed. *And then his,* he thought, before they could stick him in a concrete box.

Panic ran like ice through his veins as the world went silent. Completely, utterly silent.

A second ticked by... then, a minute.

Maybe he was crazy? Maybe he was hearing things?

"Help! In here, hellllllp!" His prisoner's shrill scream startled him.

Pop!

"No!" The other screamed.

Pop! Pop!

His mouth gaped, and he froze, staring at the convulsing women spewing blood in front of him.

BAM!

He whipped around.

BAM! The lock on the door wobbled.

His heart stopped, his breath stopped.

Do it, he thought. *Do it, you coward!* He lifted the gun to his face and inserted the barrel into his mouth. His heart skipped wildly in his chest as he turned and faced the door. He wanted the bastards to see him do it. He wanted his brain splattered all over their pig faces.

The cellar door burst open and with a grin as pure evil, he squeezed the trigger.

Click.

Bodies flew toward him. His face slammed into the cold concrete floor, pain bursting through his jaw. Blood filled his mouth.

Footsteps, shouts, it was all abuzz around him as they cuffed his hands and feet.

"Should've checked your bullets," an officer snarled in his ear.

He'd only had three fucking bullets left in the gun. Three rounds he'd just pumped into his prisoners.

As they dragged him through the door, he heard—

"Bag his gun. It's a .45 ACP. Matches the shells Wesley picked up at the range."

His eyes grew wide with fury as the memory rushed into his head.

Wesley Cross.

1

*W*ESLEY LOOKED DOWN at the blood on his hands. He hadn't bothered to wash them, hell, he hadn't even thought about it, but now he wished he'd taken a quick second to do just that.

He rubbed his thumb over his palm, a feeble attempt to erase away the dried blood.

No luck.

The coffee pot gurgled and beeped. When Chief McCord had asked him to leave the scene and wait in his kitchen upstairs, he'd started a pot. He wasn't sure why—nervous energy, he assumed. Or maybe it was a subconscious gesture to remind everyone that he was a nice guy and not someone capable of murdering his former lover in his basement. He hadn't even considered that he would be the initial suspect until he'd seen the questioning look in the Chief's eyes as he approached the scene. Wouldn't be the first time he was labeled something he wasn't. Difference was, all the other times, he didn't give a shit.

A thin beam of moonlight shone through the window above the sink, sparkling off a kitchen knife he'd used earlier in the day. A wave of nausea washed over him. He rubbed his hands together again, the blood on his skin beginning to feel suffocating.

Christ, he needed a shower.

Underneath the table, he shuffled his cowboy boots, knowing that they were covered in blood, too.

It had happened so fast. So fucking fast. The blood... just seemed to drain out of her.

He felt his pulse begin to pick up with anxiety, an unfamiliar feeling for the fearless former Marine. He glanced at the digital clock glowing from the stove—almost one thirty in the morning. The chaos in the basement was beginning to die down, but there were still a number of uniforms swarming his home. His. *Home.*

Wesley clasped his hands together on the table and swallowed the bowling ball in his throat.

"Wesley? You alright, man?"

His gaze lifted. He blinked and was pulled back to the moment. "Sorry. Yeah." He looked at the recorder sitting in the middle of the table.

"Okay." Detective Dean Walker sat across from him, a line of concern running across his tanned forehead. "We're going to go through all this again. Remember, this will all be on record now. Everything you say, okay?"

Wesley nodded.

Dean put his finger on the record button, but then paused and leaned forward. "Sure you don't need a second, man? Want to take a lap outside or something? Gather your thoughts?"

A small, appreciative smile crossed Wesley's lips. He'd always liked Dean; a hardworking, true southern cowboy, who was knee-deep in his first year as Berry Springs's only detective. Friends for decades, Dean had helped Wesley build his shop when he'd started his own gun manufacturing business eight years earlier, and Wesley had returned the favor when he helped Dean solve the cold case of Dean's father's homicide using his ballistics expertise. They respected each other, and it was a relationship Wesley was sure glad he had in his current circumstance.

"No, I want to get this shit done." He nodded toward the recorder. "Turn it on."

Dean held up a finger—*one minute*—and pushed away from the table and walked to the liquor cabinet. He returned with a half-empty bottle of Johnny Walker Blue and handed it to him. Wesley unscrewed the top, took three gulps, then passed it back. After Dean took a shot, he cleared his throat, pressed the red button on the recorder and after rattling off all the mandatory bullshit about Wesley's rights, he got to the questions.

"Let's start from the beginning. Can you tell me where you were this evening?"

"Gino's for dinner, then Frank's Bar."

"What time did you leave Frank's?"

"'Round eleven thirty."

"You go anywhere else?"

"No."

"Straight home?"

"Yes."

"What time did you get home?"

"Close to midnight."

"Notice anyone or anything strange on your property?"

"No."

"Were you looking?"

"Always." *A side effect of running special ops in the deepest depths of hell for nine years.*

"Did you pass any cars or see any parked around your house?"

"No."

"How about being followed?"

"No." He was certain of that.

"Okay, so you got home, then what?"

"I parked in my usual spot, got out and noticed the basement door was cracked open."

"You're sure you shut and locked it before you left for the evening?"

He cocked his head with a look that asked, *seriously?*

Dean glanced at the recorder.

Wesley blew out a breath. "Yes, I locked up before I left."

"Okay, go on."

"I walked inside, searched the floor and that's when I found her." His gut clenched—what he should have said was that he smelled her first, then found her. That sweet, metallic scent of blood.

He looked down and shifted in his seat.

"What condition was she in?"

Wesley's jaw twitched as he focused on a small nick in the shiny, wooden dining table. He'd built it himself out of the trunk of a massive oak tree that had fallen during last spring's storms. It had taken him two months and more splinters than he could count. The table was perfectly imperfect with uneven edges and a dozen different shades of brown. Except for tonight. Tonight, it had smears of blood on it. He looked up and narrowed his eyes. "Her throat was slashed." A heavy silence filled the room. "Fresh."

"What makes you say that?"

"She was still pink, warm. The blood was still pumping out of her neck when I walked up." He gritted his teeth and shook his head. "*Minutes*, Walker. If I had just gotten home minutes earlier..."

"Doesn't do us any good to think like that, Cross. Keep going."

Wesley nodded. "I kneeled down, looked her over, you know, and that's when I heard the upstairs door slap shut."

"Exactly how long from the moment you found her to when you heard that?"

"Maybe a minute. Maybe even less. So I went after him."

"Him?"

"Assuming, based on height, weight, and movement."

"Okay, go on."

"I ran out on the deck and saw him running through the field. Followed him into the woods, lost him for a second, then heard an engine start up." He shook his head. "Son of a bitch parked in a small clearing just off the road."

"And you didn't see a vehicle when you drove past?"

"No, there's a thick line of bushes that block the view."

"Then what?"

"He took off, and..." His defiant gaze settled on Dean's. "I shot at the fucker."

Dean's eyes flickered to the recorder. "How many shots?"

"Four."

"Where'd you hit?"

"Not sure if I did."

Dean cocked his head, narrowed his eyes. "You could hit a dove in a snowstorm. Best target shooter I've ever seen in my life. And you don't know if you hit the vehicle, at least?"

"Fucker kicked gravel in my face. I was damn near blind when I took the shots."

"Well, then, that explains why we aren't examining a dead body right now. Where'd you aim? The tires?"

"The back glass."

Dean scribbled on his notepad. "I'll have Willard call around to the area hospitals tonight. See if anyone's brought in. We'll also look for your bullet shells where he parked. What was the vehicle?"

"SUV, black."

"Make, model?"

"Thanks to the cloud of dust, I didn't get a good look. Boxy, not round. Definitely not a van."

"Who's your nearest neighbor? Any chance they saw a vehicle?"

"Old man Ericsson lives about a mile north. Closest to me. No one else lives down this road. So, no, no one else would've seen it."

"Maybe he saw an SUV on the main road, at least?"

"You mean to back up my story that I saw the suspect, and I'm not just making this up to take the focus off of myself?"

Dean stared at him a minute—*cool it.* "Alright. I've got Willard checking for tracks now. But..."

"I know, I know, not a good bet in gravel."

Dean nodded and continued his questioning. "To confirm, *her* car was *not* at your house when you got home?"

"Correct. He must've brought her in his SUV."

"What about over the course of the evening? Did you see the SUV parked anywhere you were at?"

"No."

"To confirm, you didn't see Leena earlier tonight, correct?"

"Correct."

"Did she have a key to your place?"

"No."

"Have you given a key to anyone lately?"

"No. Bobbi and my dad are the only two people who have keys."

"Where is your sister?"

"Home, safe. I called, just to make sure."

"Did you tell her what happened?"

He shook his head. "No. I will when the sun comes up."

"Good thing, considering."

"Yes, considering she'd drive her over-protective ass out here and beat down the door demanding answers." Apparently, Bobbi's reputation for being a bit high-strung preceded her.

Dean grinned.

Wesley sat back. "It's a fucking setup, Dean. Someone's setting me up."

"Who?"

"I have no idea."

"Any arguments with anyone lately?"

"No."

"What about anyone you'd done business with lately?"

"I issue background checks for every person who purchases one of my guns. Not only that, I look into them myself. Hell, I know most of the locals who've bought from me."

"Any of your guns missing?"

"I don't think so, although I'll do a full inventory tonight. Regardless, there's no way this was some robbery gone wrong. I had plenty of guns laying out, just feet from her body. And besides, why would Leena be involved?"

"Okay. Let's go back to tonight. When you found Leena in your basement, did you recognize her immediately?"

His heart skipped a beat. He'd remember that exact moment for the rest of his life. "Yes." His throat suddenly felt like it had been wiped with a fresh coat of sand. He swallowed deeply.

"Was she your girlfriend?" Dean's voice wavered.

"No, not a girlfriend."

Dean cleared his throat. "I'll need you to elaborate."

"She wasn't my girlfriend. It was casual."

"Friend with benefits?"

Wesley cocked a brow at the bluntness of the question. He shifted in his seat. "Fine. Sure. Yes, you could say that. We'd gone on a few dates. Three, I think. But that was it. We moved on."

Just then, Officer Willard opened the back door and stepped into the kitchen, his face abnormally pale, highlighted by dark circles under his green eyes. A rookie officer and son of a retired cop, Willard made an effort to always be on his A-game, but tonight, he carried the weight of seeing an almost-decapitated Berry Springs woman. Someone he very likely knew.

Dean paused the recorder. "What?"

Willard sent a nod at Wesley, then said, "No viable tracks. Nothing I can pull a cast from."

Wesley rolled his eyes.

"What about the road?"

Willard snorted, "Three cop cars, an ambulance, Jessica's car, and Wesley's truck have trampled any tracks the SUV might've left."

"Look again in the morning, and for Wesley's shells, too. Things tend to turn up in the light."

"Will do. Hayes just got to her apartment."

"Leena's?" Wesley asked.

"Yeah. Her car's there. The door was locked, and there's no sign of forced entry or struggle. Lights were off, back door was securely locked."

Dean frowned. "Purse, cell phone?"

Willard shook his head. "Hayes is searching the place now."

"Okay, check her social media accounts. We need to know every single thing this girl did and who she talked to in the last twenty-four hours. Someone knows something."

Wesley leaned forward. "Was the engine of her car cold?"

"Yes."

"So she hadn't been out in a while... she was either with someone and taken from wherever they went, or whoever killed her picked her up at home. Voluntary or forced." He looked at Dean. "Has Jessica bagged up her body yet?"

"Not sure."

"Did she see any other injuries? Bruises?"

"Not that I'm aware of right now. She'll start the autopsy ASAP, and we'll know for sure." Dean looked at Willard. "Okay. Hit Leena's accounts, see if there's any recent activity. Let me finish up here, and we'll go talk to her folks."

Wesley's heart sank. Leena Ross's parents didn't even know she was dead.

As Willard left the room, Dean shifted his attention to Wesley. "Let's get this done. We've got a long night ahead of us." He hit the record button. "You just said you and Leena had *moved on*. You guys had stopped seeing each other?"

"That's right."

"When?"

"Three weeks ago."

"Why?"

"She wanted..." He looked down. *Goddammit.* "I didn't want a full-blown relationship."

Dean nodded, as if he didn't need to ask, and was only

asking for the record. "When was the last time you spoke with her?"

Here we go. "Two days ago."

Dean's eyebrows tipped up. "What was the nature of that conversation?"

"She wanted to meet up."

"Did you?"

"No."

"Why not?"

"As I said, I didn't want a relationship."

"How'd she take that?"

He looked down again, and another unfamiliar feeling crept up—guilt. "We got into an argument."

"'Bout what?"

"That. I reiterated that I didn't want a relationship. She did, and because of that, it wasn't going to work out."

"Did she mention anything else? Any arguments with anyone else?"

"No." He'd replayed their conversation in his head a million times over the last hour.

"How'd the conversation end?"

"With her calling me a piece of shit playboy and hanging up on me."

Dean's gaze leveled on his and he knew what the detective was thinking. Getting into an argument with his former lover two days before her throat was slashed didn't bode well for him. Especially considering Leena had no doubt vented to her friends about him after the fact. Not good. There was a good chance half the town knew about their argument.

And then she turned up dead. In his basement.

Dean must've read the look in his eyes because he said, "You were on a date earlier this evening, correct?"

"Yes, first date. Blind date, set up by my sister. And I've given you Toni's number."

Dean nodded. "Yes, we've already spoken with Miss Monroe and confirmed you were with her, as well as Red up at Frank's Bar, where you went after."

"They've also got two cameras, one above the front door and one in a tree out back."

"I know."

Wesley held his gaze—s*o, I'm covered. Those are my alibis.*

~

The rumble of the last vehicle faded in the distance as Wesley pushed out the back door and stepped onto his deck, his SIG in one hand, the bottle of Walker Blue in the other. They were finally gone. *Everyone.* At three in the damn morning.

Finally.

A full moon rested on the peak of a mountain in the distance, its silver glow washing over the vast landscape ahead of him. Dark shadows stretched across the ground. A cool breeze swept past him, carrying the moldy scent of dead leaves. Fall was crisp in the air.

The seasons were changing.

He walked to the railing and gazed down at the field, its tall brown grass swaying in the wind. A thin fog was just beginning to slither above the ground.

Haunting.

Wesley took a deep breath, hoping to cleanse his body from the sickness he felt inside and the nerves squeezing his stomach. His fingers tingled as he gripped the handle of his gun, narrowed his eyes and scanned from left to right, searching for any movement in the cloud of gray. A perfect place to hide.

Come and get me, you sick son of a bitch. If you're still here, come and get me.

As if nature responded to him, a gust of wind tossed leaves across his boots. The fog moved, danced, taunting him in the breeze. He gazed out at his property. All ninety-eight acres of it.

What the *hell* had happened tonight?

Jesus Christ, *why her?*

Wesley's mind had been in a constant spin since he'd found her body in his basement. It didn't make sense. The whole thing seemed off. Someone had gone to great lengths to execute her murder. It had been carefully planned out, that much was obvious.

Who?

Why?

He glanced over his shoulder at the basement door on the side of the house. They'd dusted for prints and searched for trace evidence, but before Dean had left, he'd implied they'd found nothing useful.

There had to be something. He'd already decided that he was going to scour every inch of his place, and his property, himself. Whether they liked it or not. He'd start tonight and wouldn't stop until he found *something*.

He tipped up the bottle and chugged the smooth, amber liquid for a solid three seconds, welcoming the familiar burn down his throat. The pain before the calm. Blowing out a breath, Wesley turned toward the house and leaned against the rail, his mind reeling.

Leena's throat had been slashed no more than a few minutes before he'd found her. This meant one of two things, either the killer knew Wesley wasn't home and had poorly timed his murder, or he timed it perfectly, waiting until Wesley drove up the driveway to do it... Waited to send the knife into Leena's neck to ensure Wesley would find his former lover just seconds after death had taken her. It was a chilling thought but had much more weight to it than a random killing, or robbery gone wrong, which he didn't believe anyway. Either way, the fact that she was taken to *his* house to be killed in *his* basement screamed setup.

Why?

He turned back to the mountains. The killer had parked a good fifty yards from his house. How had he gotten Leena inside? Did she go voluntarily? If so... what the hell was she thinking? Or, was she forced? Or, drugged and dragged?

Another fact Wesley couldn't wrap his head around was that there were no apparent signs of struggle or break-in at her place.

Did she know her killer?

He didn't know of a single person who didn't like Leena. Who would do that to her?

Leena Ross was a blonde, bubbly former cheerleader, a few years younger than Wesley. They'd gone to high school together and had always flirted, but nothing more... until two months ago when she'd had one too many long island iced teas at Frank's Bar and walked right up to him and asked him out. He was surprised—shocked, really. He'd been asked out by women before, but not very often. He liked it. He liked her confidence. He said yes, and the next evening they'd gone to dinner and a movie... and to his place after. He enjoyed her company, and the sex was good, but it was like every other woman—no chemistry. No sparks.

And that pretty much summed up Wesley's dating life.

He'd begun to think something was wrong with him.

Why couldn't he commit to a woman? Or to an exclusive relationship, at least? Why couldn't he just settle? Leena Ross would've hardly been settling. She was popular in town, beautiful and single. But she was looking for a husband, that much was obvious. Her biological clock was ticking, he'd known that from the first few minutes of their first date. There had been a sparkle in her bright blue eyes, hopeful with the possibility that maybe, just maybe, he was the one.

And now, those bright eyes were forever closed.

He'd never forget looking down at her eviscerated throat, the pink flesh puffing up from her once narrow, elegant neck, now opened up like a red flower. She'd been sliced ear-to-ear. He'd seen the white bone of her spine.

Wesley tipped up the whiskey and took another gulp. His eyes watered, his throat burned.

A rush of frustration had him pushing off the rail. He clenched his jaw, grabbed the whiskey, his SIG, and began pacing. There was no way in hell he was going to be able to sleep. He had to do *something*. Something productive, something to help find the son of a bitch who'd turned his life upside down. He'd promised Dean he would inventory his guns, so that's what he'd do. After bleaching the hell out of the floor, of course. Then, he'd count his guns until he was so tired he passed out.

That's it. Make a plan, Wes.

He took one last look into the fog, then turned and began making his way across the deck, his house, dark against the shadows. *His house.* The house he'd built from scratch, the house he'd put blood, sweat, tears and every penny of his bank account into. The house that would now always be remembered as the scene of Leena Ross's murder.

Wesley had meticulously planned every inch of his

three-thousand square foot home, using all local rock and lumber. He'd purchased the land and drawn up his own blueprint even before hiring a contractor. Loyal to small-town culture, Wesley had hired only local construction workers and vendors. Along with help from his buddies, they'd constructed his house, the "Maritime Mansion" as the crew had dubbed it. The nickname was a nod to his career in the Marines although the word "mansion" didn't sit well with him. But Wesley had worked his ass off to pay for exactly what he wanted and bottom-line it was, by all counts, a very large home.

The master bedroom took up half the top floor with sweeping windows, a log-burning fireplace, reading nook, two walk-in closets, and a huge marble bathroom with windows that overlooked the mountains. The main floor was complete with a state-of-the-art kitchen, two bedrooms, an office, and a spacious living room. He operated his business, *Cross Combat,* from the basement.

Wesley had designed the sprawling deck to be a space of comfort. To celebrate the outdoors. It was a multi-level space with an outdoor kitchen, a covered seating area, and a built-in firepit. Every morning, Wesley would have coffee in the handmade lounge chairs in the morning, and cocktails in the same spot hours later. Sunrises and sunsets, each watched and appreciated.

Wesley liked to build things, to create things. He took pride in his home. This was his place, to think, to plan, to relax, to reflect. It was a safe place for him to just be himself, no matter what the day had brought him. He didn't need palm trees, the ocean, or tall, glass buildings. Only nature and lots of it. And that's exactly what he got in his hometown.

Nestled deep in the Ozark Mountains, Berry Springs

was a stereotypical small, southern town where a cowboy hat and boots were the uniform of choice and calling each other "sir" and "ma'am" was a part of daily conversation. It was a country town, with events centered around the outdoors, celebrating the dozens of hiking trails, campsites, and fishing holes in the area. Hitting up the gun range after a hard day's work was as common as heading to the bar. The monthly rodeo was a sold-out event, no matter what the weather. The town even had a country diner where locals gathered every morning for eggs, grits, and their daily dose of gossip.

This was his town, his house, and nothing was going to take that away from him.

He just had to figure out who the hell was trying to frame him for murder.

2

*W*ESLEY JERKED AWAKE at the sound of the front door slamming downstairs.

"*Wes?!*"

He groaned, cracked open his eyes, then slammed them shut at the hammer pounding between his temples.

Holy shit. He felt like shit.

"Wes?" Footsteps pounded up the staircase.

Not now, he thought. *Dear God, not right now.* He forced his eyes open again and slowly looked around the room. He remembered watching the sun rise and seeing the bottom of the whiskey bottle, and that was about it. He'd had the good sense to draw the curtains closed before passing out at... what time? Seven-thirty in the damn morning?

What time was it now?

He focused on the thin slit in the curtains. It was daytime, he knew that, but cloudy outside. Ah yes, storms were supposed to come today.

"Wesley. *Freaking.* Cross." His little sister stomped to the foot of his bed, slammed her hands onto her hips and glowered down at him. "Why the *hell* didn't you call me?"

Shit. She knew.

Wesley released another groan and sat up, the hammer feeling like a wrecking ball now. *Boom, boom, boom,* with each thump of his heart.

"What time is it?" He smacked his lips. Did he have *sand* in his mouth? *Christ* how much whiskey did he drink? Had he opened another bottle?

Bobbi walked over to the curtains and yanked them open revealing, yep, a depressingly overcast day. "It's almost noon, *Wesley.*" She turned, the anger on her face fading to anxious worry. "Wes, why didn't you call me?"

He rubbed his eyes. "I did call you and hung up."

"That was you?!"

"Yeah. Wanted to make sure you were home for the night." *And that you were safe*, he thought.

"Why didn't you tell me?"

"It was after midnight when it happened, B."

Her voice pitched as she threw her hands up in the air. "So, what? You didn't want to wake me? What the hell, Wes? Someone was murdered in your basement, and you didn't want to *wake me?*" She clenched her jaw and plopped down on the edge of the bed. Her dark brown hair was pulled into a messy bun, and even without a stitch of makeup, she was a beautiful woman. Wesley often wondered if she resembled their mother. The lack of mascara and lipstick made her look even younger than she really was, which she would never admit was twenty-nine. She was dressed in her work uniform—yoga clothes.

She shifted toward him and narrowed her eyes. "I want to know every detail. *Now.*"

Despite the knife in his brain, the corner of Wesley's lip curled up. Although Bobbi was seven years younger than him, she'd always acted like the older sibling. Hell, she acted like she was his mother. Bobbi was extremely possessive of him and had been for as long as he remembered. He loved her unconditionally and was fiercely protective of her, too. Not that she needed protection. Like him, Bobbi was a fitness buff with her own yoga studio, which he always thought was ironic because she had a temper hotter than a rattlesnake. He'd told her that, so she'd opened a shooting range right next door. Yoga and guns. That summed up his sister to a tee.

He glanced at the clock. "How the hell did you hear about it already?"

"Tammy McDowell. Walked into my sunrise yoga class asking how you were doin'. I said, what the hell, and she told me she heard they found a body in your basement. My *brother's* basement!"

His face squeezed at the decibel of her voice. "How did Tammy hear about it?"

"She used to work at the station, you know that. Probably some loose-lipped son of a bitch let it slip."

Shocker. Gossip was traded like gold in Berry Springs.

Bobbi continued, "Didn't know who it was, though. Wesley, who was it?" Her eyes rounded with panic.

"Leena."

Her jaw hit the floor. She screeched, *"Leena?!"*

That voice. Knives. Brain. He closed his eyes, raised a hand and shook his head. "Bring it down a notch, B."

"You've got to tell me everything, Wes."

"Just give me a second," he snapped. "*Jesus.*"

She looked him over. "How much whiskey did you drink last night?"

His stomach flipped at the mention of pure grain alcohol, and she must've noticed because she frowned with concern. In a much softer voice, she said, "Okay. Let me get the coffee going. Take your time coming downstairs." She laid her hand on his arm. "Hey." She leaned in. "I don't know what the hell's going on, but we'll figure this out, okay? We always do. We're Crosses. We'll fix this."

Bobbi stood, stared at him with pity for a moment, then turned and walked downstairs.

Christ.

He pressed his palms to his eyes and the image of Leena's body popped into his head. His stomach churned again. After taking a few deep breaths, Wesley ripped off the covers muttering curse words he hadn't heard since basic training and dragged himself out of bed. The cold, wood floor felt good against his clammy feet, and that's when he realized his entire body was soaked in sweat. His boxers, the only thing he had on, were drenched.

Shower. He needed a quick, ice-cold shower to bring him back to life. And toothpaste to wash the damn sand from his tongue.

Catching his reflection in the mirror, Wesley braced himself against the copper sink. As he stared back at ragged man in the mirror, a knot caught in his throat. He shook his head in disbelief of the reality he'd woken up to.

It wasn't a dream. It wasn't a nightmare. It was real.

Wesley knew nightmares could be a reality. He'd seen evil up close and personal. While running special ops for the Marines, he'd seen plenty of dead bodies, hundreds, even. Everything from burned, to mutilated, to utterly unrecognizable as a human body. It always unnerved him a bit, but over the years, he'd gotten used to it. Hardened to it, really. But this was different. He had never dated the bodies he'd seen. He'd never had sex with one of them. And he sure as hell had never found one in his home.

This kill was personal.

Against him.

His eyes narrowed, blood beginning to simmer.

No one fucks with Wesley Cross.

Fifteen minutes and one freezing-cold shower later, Wesley grabbed the first clean pair of jeans he saw, yanked a T-shirt over his slick skin and walked downstairs. His senses perked at the scent of fresh coffee brewing. He stepped into the kitchen where his sister was putting the finishing touches—spicy pickled okra—across the top of a glass filled with thick, red liquid.

"Bobbi's Bloody," he said.

She grinned. "Best Bloody Mary on the planet, and the best cure for a hangover."

She picked up the Bloody Mary in one hand and a mug filled with coffee that said *Boob Man* in the other. The mug had been a cheeky little "I'm sorry" gift she'd given him after one of their more intense arguments where she'd childishly accused him of not calling her friend back because her boobs must've not been big enough, which led into an hour-long scolding about his commitment issues.

Bobbi raised both mugs and cocked an eyebrow.

"Both," he said.

She nodded, handed him the drinks, then poured herself a cup of coffee. She leaned against the counter and sipped. "Okay, start from the beginning." Her voice low and soothing, now.

He sipped the coffee—*heaven*—and took a second to gather his thoughts as he glanced out the windows. Scattered beams of sunlight shot out from the thick cloud cover, like spotlights illuminating the bright fall colors that painted the mountains just beyond the field.

It was beautiful. Picturesque. Fall was always his favorite season.

Not this year.

Wesley took a deep breath and then dove into the horrific details of the last twelve hours of his life. Somewhere during the course of the story, Bobbi had set down her coffee and gripped the countertop with a steely look in her eyes that would have most men stammering. He knew she was doing everything in her power not to grab every gun in his house and track down the son of a bitch who'd set her brother up for murder.

"So. There's your story, Bobbi."

Bobbi released the death-grip on the counter and crossed her arms over her chest. "Does dad know?"

"No. He's still on his fishing trip in the Keys. Caught a hell of a marlin yesterday." He paused. "I don't want to tell him, B, I don't want him to worry, and I don't want to ruin his trip."

"Wes, you have to..."

"I will, once I have more information."

She nodded. A former military man, their father lacked the grace of patience, or emotions for that matter. He would undoubtedly be on the next flight out, brow-beating everyone at the station to solve Leena's murder and get the attention off his son.

Bobbi began pacing. "Who the hell... Who would do this? Do you have any idea?"

"No."

"Do the police have any leads?"

"Not as of three in the morning."

"God, Wes," she whispered. Then she asked, "Do you have any enemies? At all?"

"Enough to kill Leena in my house?"

Bobbi shrugged.

"If I did, I didn't know about it."

"Not just men. Women."

"Women?" He snorted. "No... I don't... *No*."

"Wes, no offense, but you're notorious around town for lovin' and leavin'."

"Are you suggesting a *woman*..."

"Hey, you're the first person to call women crazy."

Well, she had him there.

She continued, "What about one of your lovers' husbands—"

"Hey." He snapped. "I might be a lot of things, Bobbi, but I'm not a fucking homewrecker." He pushed off the counter, exerting the most energy he'd had all morning. Anger flashed in his puffy eyes. "I've never been with a married woman in my life. Never intend to, so don't ever insinuate that again."

Bobbi cocked an eyebrow, stared at him a beat. "It's your turn to take it down a notch, Wes."

He inhaled and muttered, "Sorry."

The cuckoo clock on the wall cackled, drawing Bobbi's attention. "*Shit.* I've got a twelve-thirty class across town."

"Old folks' home?"

She grabbed her keys. "You'd be surprised how many older women come to my class, Wes. Yoga keeps you young, and calm. You should try it sometime." She started walking to the back door.

"I know, I know, you've told me—"

Bobbi stopped in her tracks and froze. Her eyes rounded as if she'd seen a ghost.

"What? What is it, B?"

She turned to him. "I just remembered..." her voice trailed off.

"What?" He crossed the room. *"What?"*

"Well, you know Leena is, was, a regular at my Wednesday night class. Well, *holy shit*... when she came in the other day, I noticed immediately that she seemed *off*. Disheveled, kind of. So much so that I asked her what was wrong. She seemed nervous, kept glancing out the window at her car and said that she'd just had a weird couple of days."

"Weird?"

"Yeah, she used that word exactly. I asked her what she meant, and she just stared out the window and said, verbatim, 'do you ever get that feeling' and then someone interrupted us. She spent the entire rest of the class glancing out the windows."

"Do you ever get the feeling..." He repeated.

"Yeah."

A chill skirted up his spine. "... that someone's watching you."

Her eyes widened. "You're right. That's what she was going to say." She grabbed his arm. "Wes, someone had been stalking her. This wasn't random, at all."

"No, Bobbi, it wasn't. It was very carefully thought out." He looked out the window, his mind reeling.

"Leena wasn't seeing anyone was she?"

"No. She was trying to get back with me."

Bobbi took another glance at the clock, then quickly asked, "Have you heard from Detective Walker this morning?"

"That's number one on my to-do list today."

3

ING.

Kaylee picked up her phone from the bathroom counter.

Be there in five.

Butterflies tickled her stomach as she clicked out of the text message. Usually, she would have preferred to have a few drinks before taking a roll in the sheets, but unfortunately, today wasn't going to work out that way. For a split-second, she considered running to the kitchen for a quick shot of tequila but decided against it. He'd probably smell it on her breath. Not that he'd care. Not that he cared about anything about her, really, other than sex.

They'd met a few weeks earlier, at Donny's Diner of all places. She'd just finished a bottle of wine and weekly movie night with her friends when she'd popped in to get take-out. He was sitting alone in a booth and instantly caught her eye. Although older, by a decade, at least—based on the graying at his temples—he had a handsome face with sharp lines, eyes that seemed to stare into her soul, and long, dark hair that gave him a cool, mysterious vibe. When she noticed the muscles bulging under his T-shirt, she tugged down her low-cut neckline and made her move. She'd slid into the booth across from him, introduced herself and within seconds she learned that he'd just moved to town and was looking for someone to show him around, to which she offered.

One thing led to another, and she began making good on her promise by showing him around right after their dinner—right into her house. He'd left her barely able to walk at 5:07 the next morning. The man might not know a lot about Berry Springs, but he sure as hell knew his way around a woman's body. Over the next few weeks he'd come by after work, usually very late, rocked her into oblivion, and sneak out the next morning.

He intrigued her. Not just because of the thing he did with his tongue that made her toes curl, but because there was something dark about him... like a brooding musician, or something. He was even-tempered, almost emotionless.

At the sound of an engine rumbling outside, Kaylee quickly ran a comb through her blonde hair and dabbed on some peppermint flavored gloss that was supposed to plump her lips. She popped her lips and leaned closer to the mirror—nope, still no pouty, supermodel mouth. She should sue for false advertising. Kaylee stepped back from the mirror and smoothed the skin-tight cotton lounge dress she'd chosen—appropriate for a lunchtime romp. With a wink and jiggle of her breasts, she grinned and met him at the front door.

He walked inside and she frowned. Her usually stoic bed partner seemed distracted, rushed even.

"You okay?" Kaylee asked as she closed the door.

"Yes." He glanced out the window, then drew the curtains closed. "I've got... a lot to do today. Sorry."

"Look, if you've got to go..."

He turned toward her, his gaze dropping to her breasts, passion flaring in his eyes.

She flashed a flirty smile.

He gripped her waist, spun her around and heaved her body against the front door. The breath knocked out of her lungs. *Holy hell*, she was in for one hell of a ride. She felt the heat rise between her legs, loosening her up for what was to come.

He kissed her, forcing his tongue into her mouth as he ground against her. Aggressively. With one hand bracing herself on the doorknob, she wrapped the other around him, grabbing the back of his hair, yanking. Two could play this game. He was hard already, which was unusual. Usually, she had to work for it... for a while, even. With a grunt, he pulled her away from the door, swung her around and tossed her onto the couch.

She noticed him take a quick glance out the kitchen window before turning back to her. *Weird.*

With an intensity she hadn't seen before, he gripped the edges of the coffee table and tossed it to the side. Her Vogue magazines tumbled, and she bit her lip. Kaylee carefully stacked the coveted magazines every day after looking through them while sipping her morning coffee. She had every magazine from the last two years in pristine condition.

"Floor." He demanded as he unbuckled his jeans.

Kaylee cocked a brow and slid off the couch. He was naked from the waist down and on her by the time her body hit the carpet. His mouth devoured hers as he shoved up her dress, not bothering to take it off. Again, this was unusual. Thank God she'd opted against panties for this rendezvous.

Her breath caught as he shoved two fingers into her, then three, pounding her so hard her body slid upward. No preamble, no foreplay, and she felt the raw burn of dryness. She squirmed as he leaned into her neck, nipped her ear.

"Ready to get fucked?"

She gave a throaty moan, but then wondered if she really was.

"I'm not going to take it easy on you this time." His voice was low, like a growl. "Get ready."

He yanked his fingers out, grabbed her breast and squeezed, *hard,* then plunged into her. She squeezed her face at the twinge of pain. What the hell was with him today? This was the most emotion, passion, *anger,* she'd seen in him since... ever.

Was he drunk? On drugs?

He pounded her, over and over, his body slapping against hers, the friction building against her clit. Her thoughts began to fade as she melted into the carpet and let herself go. She felt a rush of wetness, opening her up to him.

Yes. There it was.

She widened her legs, tipped her head back as the heat began to turn into a spreading tingle.

"Open wider."

She did as he demanded and arched her back, letting him deeper and deeper inside her.

"That's it. You're so wet. Fuck yeah, that's it." His breathing became heavier. He released her breast and slid his hand up to her neck. But instead of gently caressing the sensitive spot behind her ear like he usually did, he lightly wrapped his fingers around her throat. Instinctively, her eyes drifted open, met his. An icy gaze pinned her, his head bobbing as he thrust into her harder, faster and faster.

She was on the edge of an orgasm, her body tightening from head to toe.

"That's it, come for me." The words came out in short gasps. He was close, too.

The pressure increased around her neck. Her thoughts clouded as her body became completely overwhelmed with sensation.

"That's it. I'm close..." she slurred out. Then her body exploded with the most intense orgasm she'd ever felt in her life, a paralyzing wave, over and over. She didn't even notice him pouring into her at the same time.

The waves stopped, and she went completely limp. Dazed, confused. An entire marching band could have walked through her house, and she wouldn't have even noticed.

He pushed off of her and stood, staring down at her. His lips were pressed in a straight line, his eyes blank.

Kaylee smiled, and between heavy breaths said, "Wow."

He nodded. "Good."

"Did you?"

He nodded.

Kaylee pushed up on her elbows as he slid on his clothes. He was quiet and in a hurry. Why? What was going on?

She watched him pull keys from his pocket and step to the front door. He put his hand on the knob, paused and turned.

"Will you swing by tomorrow?" He asked.

"That's the plan."

He nodded. "I'll see you tomorrow night, then."

ESLEY PARKED IN-BETWEEN a jacked-up truck with two hunting dogs panting in the bed, and a dually with an American flag attached to the antenna. Donny's Diner was packed, not that it surprised him. The diner was busy from the moment it opened its doors at five a.m. to the moment it closed. He glanced at the clock—1:02. Apparently, the entire town had shown up for lunch.

He slid his SIG, the gun he always carried with him, into its holster underneath a worn plaid button-up that he'd thrown over his T-shirt. It was a cloudy fall day, sitting steadily in the mid-sixties. The afternoon had grown completely overcast.

The smell of sizzling bacon and fresh coffee welcomed him as he pushed through the glass doors. One of his favorite things about the south was that bacon was an acceptable side dish no matter what time of day it was. His stomach growled, which was a hell of a lot better than the flip-flops it had been doing since he awoke. Progress.

"Well, howdy there, Wesley!" Carrying a tray packed to

the edges with steaming plates and mugs of coffee, Mrs. Booth paused in front of him.

He wiped his cowboy boots on the *Howdy* mat and smiled. "Hi, Mrs. Booth. Crowded today."

She glanced past him, out the window. "Folks comin' in before the storm hits."

"Supposed to be big?"

The waitress nodded, her thick-rimmed glasses bobbing on top of her gray hair, knotted in a bun with a yellow number-two pencil. "*Storms*, I should say. Don't you watch the weather, boy? Supposed to be gettin' some really bad weather over the next two days. Thunderstorms and bad floodin'. Stan the Weatherman even mentioned the possibility of a tornado."

"Tornadoes, huh?"

"Yep. Always busy before bad weather. Well, better get these passed out before Mr. and Mrs. Boone pull a shotgun on me like they did to their daughter's boyfriend last week."

Wesley grinned. Mrs. Booth worked seven days a week and served up as much gossip as she did coffee. Apparently, though, the news of the latest dead body in Berry Springs hadn't reached her. Thank God.

She started to walk away, but paused, "Hey, congrats on that big government contract you signed. Hear you're rollin' in the money now, son."

Son. "Thanks. It's keeping me busy, that's for sure." He scanned the diner.

"Who ya lookin' for?"

"Dean..."

"Back corner, the usual. Be right there to get your order."

"Thanks, Mrs. Booth."

Wesley spotted the detective in an intense conversation on his cell phone. Officer Willard sat across from him, scrolling through his phone. Wesley walked up as Dean tossed the phone on the table. His eyes were puffy, his brown hair messy and his face pale—the typical appearance for any detective after working a homicide all night.

"Hey, Wesley. Have a seat."

Willard scooted over in the red booth and without looking up from his phone, muttered, "Hey, man."

"Hey." He slid into the booth.

Dean blankly stared out the window, his thoughts obviously a million miles away. After a moment, he said, "Bad weather coming."

"So I hear. Chance of tornadoes, according to Mrs. Booth."

Dean shook his head and looked at the waitress scurrying across the room. "Thank God that's the only news she's spreading today."

"Won't take long. Bobbi already heard about it."

"Ah, *hell*."

Willard clicked off his phone, finally joining the conversation. "Won't matter anyway. It'll be out before too long. Lanie Peabody from NAR news already left me a voicemail. Only knows *something* happened last night. Probably heard the commotion over the scanner."

Dread crawled like ants over Wesley's skin. Shit was going to hit the fan when the news broke that his former lover was found with her throat slashed in his basement. The small town would be buzzing with theories, most involving his name. Just the thought made him want to skip town for a few days. Not because of the gossip, but because he didn't want it to affect his family and business.

"Alright boys," Mrs. Booth walked up, yanking a pencil from behind her ear. "What can I get Berry Springs's finest... and Wesley," she winked.

Dean handed her his menu. "Tuna melt, fries, and sweet tea. Please, ma'am."

Willard nodded. "Exact same."

Wesley glanced down at the menu. After a quick debate, he went with ol' faithful. "Chili cheeseburger, extra cheese, fries, and sweet tea." Greasy food to even out his blood sugar.

Willard cocked an eyebrow.

"And a brownie," he added, looking at the rookie.

Willard laughed.

Mrs. Booth scribbled on her notebook and grinned. "Two tuna melts, and one cure for the hangover, comin' right up."

The waitress walked away. Wesley leaned back. "Is it really that obvious?"

Dean and Willard glanced at each other. They didn't need to respond, Wesley knew he looked like shit. Dog shit. But that was the least of his worries. He looked at Dean and got down to business. "First things first. I inventoried my shop—all guns accounted for, so we can let go of the robbery gone wrong theory, which made no fucking sense anyway."

"Good. Thanks for getting that done so quickly."

"What've we got so far?"

Dean blew out a breath and checked his phone as if willing an update to come through at that moment. "Nothing concrete. We did get the results back on your doorknob. No prints, but they found traces of latex."

"He wore gloves."

"Exactly. Which gives us jack shit, other than confirming he broke in." Dean shook his head. "I can't believe you don't double lock your basement. Anyone could've broken in that door. Hell, whoever did it probably used a damn credit card."

Maybe Dean was right, but Wesley had never worried too much about security on his property. He had over a hundred guns in his house and was lethally trained in hand-to-hand combat. Hell, *he* was a walking security system.

"Anything new with her apartment?"

"No," Willard said. "Like I said last night, no sign of a break in, a struggle or anything suspicious so far."

"Security cameras?"

"No."

"What about her neighbors? They see or hear anything?"

"Not a damn thing. She lives in a four-unit building. One unoccupied; the couple in another were out for the evening, and yes, I've verified that, and the elderly woman in the fourth unit says she didn't see or hear anything, although I don't think she can hear very much if you catch my drift."

Dean chimed in. "We've got Leena on camera leaving the grocery store at seven-fifteen last night, that's it. Best we can tell she went home, put up the groceries, and that's where the trail ends."

"Still no purse or cell?"

"No. Whoever took her tossed them probably. The cell's off. We're going through the red tape to get her call and text log. Hoping for that by tomorrow, the latest."

"Goddamn red tape." Wesley sighed, then said, "What did her folks say?"

Willard stiffened next to him, and Dean shifted in his seat before looking at him.

Wesley narrowed his eyes. "What?"

Mrs. Booth delivered their teas, and picking up on the

sudden tension, lingered a moment before walking away. Wesley's eyes didn't leave Dean.

Willard broke the silence. "They mentioned you."

"What?"

Dean shot Willard an icy glare.

"They mentioned *me?*" He looked at Willard, who was avoiding eye contact by stirring sugar into his tea, then back at Dean. "You weren't going to tell me? What did they say?"

"Look, Wesley. I've got no doubt you had nothing to do with this. Hell, you've got an ironclad alibi. But that doesn't mean people aren't gonna talk. To answer your question, no, I wasn't going to tell you. You've got enough on your shoulders right now."

"What the fuck did they say?" He enunciated each word, his voice colored with impatience and anger.

Dean took a deep breath. "Apparently, Leena had mentioned y'alls argument the other day. Was very upset, so they say. I guess… she liked you a hell of a lot more than you realized, man."

The mountain of guilt he was already feeling tripled.

"She told them you seemed agitated with her. I guess because she couldn't move on or something."

"Wait… are you saying they insinuated that I might have something to do with it?"

Dean's gaze leveled on him. In a no-bullshit tone, he said, "Yes. Her father did, yes."

"You told them about my alibis, right?"

"Of course. But, the thing is, according to them, they couldn't think of a single person who had anything against her. She was really well-liked around town. She wasn't seeing anyone; no arguments with friends, nothing. No arguments lately, except for with you."

Wesley clenched his jaw and inhaled to unload his frustration when Mrs. Booth, with her impeccable timing again, delivered their food. He grabbed his burger and took a bite. A second, a pause, to calm down.

Willard popped a fry into his mouth. "And that's that part of it." An obvious attempt to move the conversation along. "Her mom also said that she'd spoken with Leena on the way to the grocery store last night, around six-forty-five. Said Leena said she'd just planned to stay home and catch up on laundry. She had no plans with anyone."

Dean nodded. "So, if that's true, it's less likely that someone she knew came over."

"Unless it was a drop-in."

"True. We've also spoken with her closest friends, Sara Brown and Morgan Clark." Dean slid a glance at Wesley.

"*No,* I haven't slept with either of them, you son of a bitch."

Dean grinned, shrugged, then continued. "They both confirmed what her mom said. Leena didn't have any plans with anyone last night. Best we can tell right now, Leena Ross was abducted from her apartment, taken to your house, and murdered to set you up." He narrowed his eyes. "It's about you, not her."

Dean's and Willard's gazes laid heavily on him for what felt like a solid ten seconds. He forced himself to chew his food and not throw it up. He knew it, and he'd known they knew it, but hearing the words made it real.

Leena Ross died because of him.

"It could have been anyone, then? Any woman? Is that what you're saying? Whoever I was last involved with?"

"That's my gut reaction. Hell, Wesley, it's the only thing that makes sense." Dean leaned forward. "Now we need to figure out why. Who the hell's setting you up, and why?"

Dean and Willard picked up their tuna melts and dug in.

Wesley took another bite, needing a moment to choose his next words carefully. After a few minutes, he set down his burger and said what had been rolling around his head since Bobbi told him that Leena implied she'd been followed.

"It might not be a cut-and-dry setup. Think about it. No one would go to the effort of kidnapping someone I had a relationship with, drag her to my house and kill her without making sure I was somewhere that couldn't be confirmed. They'd make sure I didn't have an alibi, right? Bobbi said Leena had been acting odd at yoga Wednesday night, kept looking out the windows. The killer had been watching her, more than likely me too. He'd planned this out for days, potentially. He knew I wasn't home and probably knew exactly where I was—around dozens of people and multiple security cameras." He paused, narrowed his eyes. "It's not a setup, guys. It's a message. Someone's fucking with me."

A heavy silence settled around the booth. Finally, Dean slowly nodded. "It's a possibility. But, again, Wesley, who? Why?"

"No clue."

"*Think*, Wesley. Anyone you've pissed off lately? Work-related, even? Shit, could be someone from high school, maybe? Maybe someone jealous?"

Willard cut him a glance. "Woman related?"

"Why the fuck does everyone think that?"

"Dude, come on, now's not the time to beat around the bush. We're looking at everything."

"Listen," his tone sharp, "I know I've got a reputation as a bit of a cocky ladies' man—"

Dean snorted.

Wesley glared, then continued, "But I've always been

respectful to women. I've never strung anyone along, and I've always been honest."

"Honest that you don't care to settle down?"

"Yes. Always."

Willard cocked his head, a thoughtful expression on his face. "Why is that?"

Wesley shifted in his seat. "What is this, fucking Oprah?"

Willard chuckled.

Dean didn't. "Well, buddy, it might feel like Oprah shortly. I met with the Chief an hour ago, and he wants you to come by the station if you can. Considering that it appears that the motive for Leena's murder is all on you, he'd like you to answer some more questions, on the record. It'll be no pressure, no heat."

He nodded. He'd expected as much. "Anything you need, Dean."

"Thanks. We'll make it as quick and painless as possible."

Wesley mindlessly stirred his tea. "Where's Leena... I mean, her body, now?"

"Jessica's got her. She started the autopsy this morning." Dean glanced at his cell. "I told her to call the minute she has any information..."

Just then, behind them, "How about a face-to-face instead?"

Wesley turned to see the vivacious, redheaded, green-eyed medical examiner step up to the table. Jessica Heathrow was not only notorious for her infallible competency when it came to dissecting dead bodies, but also for her ball-busting attitude, and ability to cuss any man under the table. Wesley had liked her the moment they'd met when they were little kids.

Dean's eyebrows tipped up as he scooted over in the booth. "Speak of the devil."

Jessica slid in next to him. "I just went by your office. They said you'd come here to grab a bite to eat and Lord knows I'd never pass up a meal at Donny's."

Wesley pushed his plate across the table. "Eat. My stomach's not..."

"Doing well since you found a dead body in your basement?" Jessica ripped the corner off a napkin, pulled a massive wad of bright pink gum out of her mouth and wrapped it up.

Willard wrinkled his nose. "What is that? Bubblicious?"

"Yep. Watermelon. Got a problem with that?"

"No, not at all. Watermelon was my favorite... in 1985."

"Ha. Ha." She grabbed the burger and took a bite. With a mouthful, she looked at Wesley and asked, "Seriously, how you doing?"

"A lot better if you've got any information to move this damn thing forward."

Jessica swallowed and looked around the table at the intense stares aimed at her. She grabbed Wesley's drink, sipped, then cleared her throat. "I confirmed the cause of death was cardiac arrest due to rapid blood loss."

"Cardiac arrest?"

"Yes." Jessica grabbed a napkin and wiped her mouth. "There's two ways to die from a sliced throat. If only the trachea is cut, the victim dies from lack of oxygen or from blood flowing through the laceration into the lungs. Kind of like drowning. Not fun. Now, if the carotid arteries are cut, blood loss is the cause. Sometimes, only one gets severed, which is a slower death. In Leena's case, both arteries were severed, along with the trachea."

Both Dean and Willard set down their tuna melts.

"This tells me two things, potentially. The killer is strong, and/or, he knows what he's doing. Meaning, he's done this before."

"Why do you assume he's strong?"

"To cut through both arteries and the trachea takes some pressure. He'd had to have restrained her as well. And it implies he knows what he's doing—how to kill with the most impact."

Wesley remembered seeing the bone of Leena's spine through her throat. "Or, anger, right? Rage? Rage can give someone abnormal strength. I've seen it."

"Me, too. And with every victim I've examined that linked back to rage, he or she was beaten badly before, and in some cases after. She wasn't." She continued, "So the good news with Leena is that she died quickly. Probably passed out within a few seconds, officially died maybe a minute later. If only one artery had been cut, it would've been longer."

In a grim voice, Willard muttered, "Silver-lining."

Jessica bit into Wesley's chili cheeseburger, the red sauce dripping onto the plate. Wesley, Willard, and Dean looked away simultaneously.

Dean leaned forward. "Based on your assessment that Leena's death doesn't appear to be personal, it furthers our theory that this one-hundred percent has to do with Wesley."

She lifted a shoulder. "Just telling you what I've found so far."

"What else?" Wesley asked.

"I can confirm your killer cut her from behind and is left-handed. The piercing is the deepest on her right side, and gradually lessens as the knife was dragged across."

"How do you know she was cut from behind?"

"The angle of the cut, and the bruising on her right bicep. He was behind her. Can almost see his grip, and the bruising is concurrent with the time of death."

"Any bruising anywhere else?"

"No, but she has a small—I'm talking teeny-tiny—laceration just between her seventh and eighth rib. Barely pierces the skin."

Dean raised his eyebrows. "So she was possibly kidnapped at knifepoint."

Wesley nodded. "And forced to go to my place, then forced across the field to the basement."

"But in whose car?"

"Whoever drives a dark SUV." Wesley's gaze leveled on Jessica. "No other injuries at all?"

"No. She wasn't sexually assaulted, if that's what you're asking."

Wesley surprised himself by releasing an audible exhale. *Thank God.*

"But, hang on, I'm not done..."

He went still, and she continued. "I did find something interesting..." she cleared her throat as if taking a second to gather her thoughts. "Well, in the incision on her throat..." She cleared her throat again. "I found maggots."

"*Maggots?*"

"Well, not actual maggots. Eggs. Insect eggs."

Dean's brow furrowed. "What the—"

"Yeah, my thoughts exactly. I actually said those exact words the moment I noticed it. Obviously, she hadn't been dead long enough for insects to crawl inside and lay eggs, so yeah..." she reached up and scratched her head. "It was an interesting find." She looked at Wesley. "So, unless you've got nasty, rotting carcasses in your basement..."

Wesley's confused expression matched Dean's. "No, of course not. Are you sure?"

"I'm always sure."

"But, how? How is it possible?"

"Hey, it's not my job to figure that out. I just tell y'all what I find, you go figure it out."

"Wait..." Willard cocked his head. "Don't flies lay eggs that turn into maggots? Isn't that what a maggot is? Eggs from a fly?"

"Yeah, I mean, I'm no bug expert, but yeah."

"Couldn't a fly have just landed on her and laid the eggs?"

Jessica shook her head. "No. Dude, she'd only been dead minutes before Wesley found her. *And,* the eggs were deep inside the wound. If it had happened as quickly as it would've had to, the eggs would have been on top."

Baffled, Wesley stared blankly back at her.

Jessica took another bite, chewed a minute, then said, "It's interesting for sure. Worth looking into but that's just my two cents."

Dean nodded. "We need an entomologist."

"*Forensic* entomologist," Jessica corrected.

"I think the state crime lab contracts that out. Not too many around here." He looked up with a grim look on his face. "Definitely won't be a fast process."

Wesley vehemently shook his head. "No way. We need this done *now*. Like, today." He looked at Jessica who had moved onto the fries. "Who's the best around?"

"Best what?"

"Forensic ento... whatever."

She snorted. "You won't get her."

"Name?"

"Seriously, Wesley, she's busy as hell. Travels the country

giving lectures when she's not working a case." She grinned. "She's not really your type of gal, anyway."

His eyebrows tipped up. "What the hell's that supposed to mean?"

"She eats guys like you for breakfast."

"Guys like me?"

She flashed a devilish smirk, "Yeah, cocky, alpha, can't-take-no-for-an-answer kind of guys."

Willard chuckled.

She continued, "You'll never get her. She's self-employed, does contract work all over the world. No way in hell you guys can afford her. The department will never cover that cost. You'll have to wait for the state—

"I'll pay for it." Wesley grabbed his phone. "What's the name, Jess?"

Jessica huffed out a breath. "Gwyneth Reece."

5

G WEN HIT A pothole, bouncing her out of her seat. She heard the *thump* of the bottom of her rental car hitting a rock. She ground her teeth and gripped the steering wheel. Was she even on a road? She looked down at the row of grass running through the middle of tire tracks.

A few miles down a "dirt road," they'd said.

This was more of a trail. Not a stay-at-home-mommy-jogging-with-her-fancy-stroller kind of trail, no, this was a here's-the-money-where's-my-fucking-drugs kind of trail.

Gwen glanced at the GPS on her console. She was going in the right direction, right? Shouldn't she be there by now? She'd put in the coordinates correctly, hadn't she? Maybe the GPS had short-circuited. After all, "there" was a tiny speck hidden deep in the Cascade Mountains, in some of the most treacherous terrain in the Northwest.

As if setting the scene, the waning light of dusk cast deep shadows around her, darkening the forest with each passing minute. Tiny droplets blurred her windshield. It wasn't rain or drizzle, but a relentless mist. Like a fog, except wetter.

Gwen scanned the woods. Thousands and thousands of deep green firs spearing against the muted fall colors of the underbrush. She'd never seen trees so tall, or so close to a "road." She'd eventually given up on worrying about the branches swiping—no doubt scratching—the little, tomato-red Prius that the airport had rented her. She had much more important things to worry about.

Like what kind of nightmare awaited her at the end of this journey.

Gwen slowed the car—not that she needed to. She hadn't passed a single vehicle in forty-five minutes—and released one hand from the steering wheel. Keeping one eye on the road, she shuffled through the papers in the brown manila envelope on the passenger seat and found the directions to the site in her barely legible scribbles just below the name *Eva Mancuso*. She read off the coordinates and doubled checked the GPS. Yep, she was on the right track—assuming the ancient-looking device was accurate.

What if it wasn't?

If something happened to her out here, would anyone even find her?

Gwen turned on the headlights. There was enough light to see for the moment, but she wanted the comfort of the extra light. A false comfort, but comfort nonetheless.

Her fingers anxiously tapped the steering wheel, and she reached down and fiddled with the radio. *Crackle, crackle, crackle... crackle, crackle* was all she got.

Gwen blew out a breath, feeling the queasiness that accompanied exhaustion. It had been a hell of a day. Twenty-four hours, really. She'd spent most of the evening polishing off a six-pack while catching up on the mountain of work she was behind on. Five hours later, she received a call from the FBI, and after spending the remainder of the evening studying the regional insect fauna of Oregon, she'd booked the first flight out, packed up, and hightailed it to the airport, where her plane had been delayed due to weather. Storms, apparently. The delay she could handle, but the hairy, drunk, beast of a man she was seated next to when she'd finally boarded ate up her last bit of patience. Especially when he'd snored like a foghorn the entire flight. She'd landed in Colorado for her layover, and was delayed, yet again.

It had been a full day of travel from her hometown of Austin, Texas, to the tiny town of Mount Hood, Oregon.

Gwen clicked on her high beams and squinted at the small clearing ahead. Her lights bounced off the red reflective tail lights of a truck.

Praise the Lord. She'd reached her destination.

Three more vehicles and a black van crowded the clearing. The CSI team was already there. She was probably the last person to arrive. Gwen parked off to the side, half-way in a ditch. After grabbing her flashlight, coat, and bag, she pushed out of the car.

The air was wet and thin, squeezing her chest with each inhale. What elevation had she climbed to? She set her bag on the hood, slipped on her all-weather jacket and pulled her long, brown hair—a ball of frizz now—back in a bun. According to the email she'd printed out, she should see a trail leading through the trees. But if it was anything like the "road" she'd been on, the "trail" might be no more than a few twigs snapped off. She followed boot tracks in the mud to, not surprisingly, a barely-there pathway cutting through the forest. After clicking on her flashlight, Gwen descended into the woods. Her final destination should be about a quarter mile past the clearing where she'd parked, at the edge of a ravine.

Gwen glanced up at the dimming sky, the stars just beginning to twinkle. It would be completely dark by the time she arrived.

She shook her head. *Just perfect*.

A cold gust of wind blew past her. She zipped up her jacket as she glanced into the darkening woods, a feeling of unease gripping her. Shouldn't she be able to hear them? Muffled voices in the distance, at least?

In an effort to dispel the desolation, Gwen focused on her footsteps, the pine needles crunching beneath her feet, knowing that each step taking her closer to seeing an actual human being... and a dead one. She listened to the sounds of nature around her and zeroed in on the insects, naming each one by the sound of their chirp. A game. A carefree game to pass the time while she walked alone through the middle of the woods.

Just then, leaves rustled behind her. She spun on her heel expecting to see either a massive bear or a serial killer.

But there was nothing. Just a rocky trail that faded into darkness.

Geez, she was abnormally jumpy. Perhaps from lack of sleep. Perhaps from that six-pack she'd drunk before bed.

She pressed on.

Minutes ticked by and finally, beams of fluorescent light cut through the trees in the distance.

Thank. God.

Renewed energy had her pace quickening. She'd never been so happy to hear voices before in her life. The path took a curve and the scene opened up around her. Multiple klieg lights circled a small clearing, illuminating the ground as if it were a stage. The fog looked like a cloud under the bright lights, slowly swaying over the scene. Beyond the big spotlight on the ground, total darkness. She counted six people, each with navy-blue jackets with *FBI* written in bright yellow across the back. Two on their knees hovering over a lump on the ground, three slowly scanning the area with flashlights, and one on his cell phone. A German Shepherd, also wearing an FBI vest, barked at her arrival and a few heads lifted, locking on her as she stepped out of the woods.

"Miss Reece."

A short, stocky man with a shaved head stepped out of the woods, with a flashlight in his hand and a hard look on his face—a look she'd seen many times before.

"Yes."

"I'm Agent Stein. Thanks for coming on such short notice."

"Not a problem." She received a firm handshake from fingers that felt like a leather belt.

He pulled a notebook from his pocket. "I'm going to need you to sign here, please."

She scribbled her name on the crime scene log.

"Thanks." He tucked the notebook back into his pocket, and they fell into step together.

"A couple of hunters found her this morning," he said. "Called it in immediately, and they called us."

"No official ID yet?"

He shook his head.

"And you think it's possibly related to the Caregiver Killer?" A horrific name created by the media, she thought.

"A possibility, yes."

A *good* possibility. She'd read the report.

Over the last two months, a deranged serial killer had murdered three elderly women, each taken from various nursing homes or assisted living facilities within a sixty-mile radius. Each a petite woman with mental illness. Each brutally sexually assaulted with various tools, then strangled to death, their bodies found weeks later in remote areas of the Cascade Mountains. Three bodies found, two still missing, one named Eva Mancuso. The story had made national news. After the second body had been found, the local police passed the case to the state, who promptly engaged the FBI. After weeks of investigating false leads, dead-ends, and chasing their tails, the federal agents were no closer to pinning down the killer. Due to the state the latest body found was in, Gwen had received a call.

He continued, "The body is short. Very short."

"How tall is Eva?"

"Five-two."

"And how long has Eva been missing?"

"Forty-nine days."

Forty-nine days. *Shit.*

A moment passed, then Stein said, "She's not in good shape."

"How do you mean?"

"Advanced decay."

"You said she. I'm assuming you know it's a female from the pelvic bone?"

"Exactly. Also, her bones show advanced osteoporosis, and short gray hair is still attached to the skull."

"An elderly woman. It's got to be her."

He clenched his jaw and nodded.

"Injuries?"

"To the pelvic region, you mean?"

She slowly nodded.

"Yes." His tone was as cold as ice. "Knife marks on the bone."

Gwen's gut clenched. Although she'd seen countless numbers of dead bodies, countless murdered victims, sexual assault was something she never got used to. Never accepted.

"Clothing?" She asked.

"No."

Her gaze fixed on the carcass between the two agents who hovered over it as they walked up.

Agent Stein cleared his throat. "Agent Mackenzie, Dr. Perez, this is Gwyneth Reece, our forensic entomologist."

Agent Mackenzie looked over her shoulder, surprising Gwen with stunning green, almond-shaped eyes and a beautiful smile. Gwen had been to plenty of crime scenes and stunning and beautiful usually weren't the words she'd use to describe the agents. Ninety-percent of the time, she worked with men; older men with frown lines and bags under their eyes, a chronic side effect of spending twenty-four hours a day working homicides.

"Miss Reece, pleasure to meet you. Your reputation precedes you."

Gwen smiled and shifted her attention to a dark-haired man who'd yet to acknowledge her presence. He'd been introduced as a doctor, and Gwen assumed he was the forensic medical examiner.

Agent Mackenzie gave a subtle eye roll at his dismissal of the new girl. "*Perez.* This is Gwyneth Reece."

Without looking up, he said, "Haven't heard of her."

Gwen's brow lifted. *Fantastic.* Another overworked, cocky, male chauvinist. She was definitely used to that. Due to her age and the fact that she had a vagina, men in her field didn't take her seriously. Of the ninety-percent she crossed paths with, eighty-five were assholes. Some sexist, some jealous of her accolades, but most jealous of her bank account. Being self-employed, she made triple what government and city employees made. In some cases, quadruple.

Well, Dr. Dickhead was going to have to get over whatever issue he had with her because she was here to get a job done, and nothing was going to stand in the way of that.

She grabbed two latex gloves from her bag and slid them on as Mackenzie updated her.

"Based on how decomposed the victim is, we're thinking she's at least a month deceased, more than likely longer. Hoping you can nail down a tighter timeframe."

Gwen nodded. The longer a body decomposed, the fewer insects inhabited it, making her job much harder to pull a solid analysis, especially when the body had been exposed to the elements the entire time.

But it wasn't impossible.

Dr. Dickhead stood, yanked off his gloves and stretched his back. "Don't see any bugs." He finally looked at her. "You've got your work cut out for you."

She met his gaze, narrowed her eyes. "I like a challenge."

"Have at it, then."

"Can I move her freely?"

He nodded, then turned to Agent Stein. "Coffee in the van?"

"Just brewed it."

"Perfect. Be right back."

The doctor limped away, and for a split-second, Gwen had sympathy for the man. He was probably one of the first people on the scene and had been bent over a rotted corpse for hours upon hours, searching for the most minute piece of evidence that could finally nail down the Caregiver Killer.

Agent Mackenzie peeled off her gloves, too. "Coffee actually sounds good. Temperature's dropped about ten degrees with the sun. You want some?"

"No, thanks. Had a gallon on the plane."

"Alright, then. I'll be back in a sec."

Mackenzie walked away as Agent Stein lingered a moment. "Sorry, Dr. Perez is—

"It's fine." She kneeled down, already forgetting about Dr. Dickhead as her mind switched to analytical.

"Good." His phone rang, and he stepped away.

Finally, she was alone. Just the way she liked it.

A line of concentration ran down her forehead as she looked at the remnants of what used to be a woman. Agent Stein said the body was in advanced decay, and he was right. At this stage in decomposition, animals had eaten ninety-percent of the organs and skin. Only a few scraps remained on the brittle gray bones, which were covered in small teeth marks. Strands of stringy gray hair clung to the skull, which was completely devoid of tissue. Black holes stared at her from where the eyes had been. The jaw was stretched open as if she'd died mid-scream. Gwen had seen enough dead bodies to recognize the sex from the bone structure alone. This woman had a small jaw, high cheekbones, and petite frame. She bet she'd been beautiful.

The grass that surrounded the corpse was dead, colored brown from the fluids that had drained from the body. Below the torso, she noticed a decent amount of dry flesh still attached to the bottom of the corpse. Hope shot through her. Maybe she'd find something useful after all.

Gwen recorded the temperature of the air and soil, humidity, elevation, and details of the body, then took multiple samples of the soil and vegetation around the body. Finally, with the utmost delicacy, she slid her fingers under the body—

"Need help?" Agent Mackenzie squatted next to her.

"Sure, thanks. If you can carefully lift here..."

Mackenzie slowly lifted the pelvic bone. "What are you doing?"

Gwen slid onto her stomach. "Soil samples."

Mackenzie watched her for a moment. "I've got to be honest with you. When they said they'd called in an entomologist, I was surprised. I thought the body had to be relatively fresh, riddled with insects and organisms to get an accurate time of death."

"That's definitely optimal." She scooped some soil into a vial. "But regardless of the state, you'd be surprised how much insects can tell us about a body."

"Even this body?"

She nodded. "For time of death, I use one of two methods: insect succession and maggot development. For bodies longer than a month deceased, like this one, I use insect succession."

"Meaning... analyzing the stages of the bugs that inhabited the body, right?"

"Exactly. Each stage of decomposition attracts and supports different species of insects."

"So you're taking soil samples to find their shells or whatever."

"Exactly. Pupae and pupal cases."

"Flies?"

"And beetles. In this particular scenario, I'm looking for beetles as much as fly cases."

"Beetles?"

Gwen glanced up, a wicked smile on her face. "Ever heard of the bone beetle?"

Mackenzie shook her head.

"Google it... some interesting videos. They feed not only on larvae but flesh, too."

"Gross."

Gwen chuckled as she scooped the final sample into a vial. She pushed up and secured the vials in her bag. "Keep holding it up if you can; I'd like to take a quick look underneath." She grabbed her flashlight and magnifying glass and slid back down.

She frowned, cocked her head. "*No way,*" she muttered. She scooted closer, peering into the magnifying glass.

"What do you see?" Mackenzie leaned down next to her.

Keeping her eyes on the soil, Gwen reached back into her bag, felt around and grabbed tweezers and another vial.

"Lift just a bit higher." Carefully, she plucked the tiny bugs from the bottom of the corpse, and then sat up. "The bottom of this corpse is covered in drain flies."

Mackenzie cocked her head. "Drain flies?"

"Yes."

"Okay... you seem surprised?"

"Yeah." Eyebrows knitted in deep thought, she gazed up at the sky, then back at the agent. "Well, I wouldn't be surprised by a few... but this many..." She looked into the woods, her mind racing.

"Why? Are you sure they're drain flies? I thought blowflies..."

Gwen shook her head. "No, these are drain flies." She handed Mackenzie the vial and magnifying glass and shone the flashlight. "See? Look very closely."

"They look like moths... a tiny moth."

"Exactly. Adult drain flies look a lot like moths. They have a dark gray body and lightly colored wings, and are fuzzy in appearance, like a moth."

"Why does them being here surprise you?"

"Drain flies aren't uncommon, but hanging out under a dead body is surprising. Especially this amount. They typically live around drain systems, hence the name. They feed on raw, organic material. Standing water, mold, etcetera. They're hell in homes. Common. But out here? In the mountains, around all this fresh, running water? This many?" She shook her head. "No, I wouldn't assume there would be this many in one place... aside from a sewage plant or something."

"Did you say sewage plant?" Stein asked.

She turned to see Dr. Perez and Agent Stein, who had apparently been behind her the entire time. "Yes." She looked back and forth between the two, who were staring at her with an expression that had her straightening. "Yes. A sewage plant."

The men exchanged a glance, and she looked back at Mackenzie, whose wide eyes shifted from the doctor, back to her, and then said, "The first nursing home where a woman went missing, two months ago... the janitor at the facility also works at the local sewage plant. We interviewed the entire staff, twice."

Gwen's eyebrows shot up as Dr. Perez kneeled down and said, "What did you say your name was again?"

"Gwyneth Reece."

He thrust out his hand. "You might've just solved this case for us."

6

*W*ITH HER CELL phone clenched in her mouth, her bag and purse slung over her shoulder and a greasy sack of fast-food in one hand, Gwen kicked the door closed behind her. Feeling like her back was about to snap in half, she walked to the king-sized bed and dumped everything on the wool Navajo-print comforter. She blew out a breath and stretched her neck from side-to-side and then looked around the room that cost her two-hundred and fifty dollars.

The Deer's Den was a small, boutique hotel that reminded her more of a bed and breakfast. Quaint and cozy. Located in the small village of Mount Hood, Oregon, it was exactly what you'd expect from the name. A log-cabin themed hotel nestled in the foothills of the mountains, with a massive wood-burning fireplace in the lobby and deer heads mounted on the walls. She'd gotten the last room available, minutes after word had spread that another body had been found.

Gwen locked the door and glanced out the window where a small group had gathered in the parking lot, a few looking right into her room. Apparently, the locals had already pinned her as involved in the investigation. Media vans with cigarette smoke rolling out the windows filled the small parking lot. Eager, anxious reporters waiting for the next briefing.

She drew the curtains as her phone beeped, alerting her to another voicemail.

Another freaking voicemail.

No reception at the crime scene meant peace and quiet, but when she'd made it back to civilization, she had seventeen missed calls and six voicemails. None of which she'd checked.

The phone beeped again, and she glanced at the clock—11:51 p.m. She looked at the greasy bag of chicken fingers. Food first. And maybe a drink.

A shiver caught her as she slid out of her muddy jacket. Although it was fall, the northwest evenings still dipped in the forties, nothing like the mild temperatures back in Texas. Gwen toe-heeled out of her hiking boots, which were also packed with mud, then padded across the room and yanked open the minibar, fully stocked.

Nice job, Deer's Den.

She wiggled her fingertips across each bottle, carefully considering her selection, then decided on a beer. Nothing like an ice-cold beer to end the day with.

Gwen popped the top, took a long sip and sank onto the bed. Her feet ached, her back ached. Her whole body felt sore with exhaustion.

You need a vacation, were the last words her mom said to her during their last conversation, and maybe she was right. Maybe she needed some time off. Everyone took vacations, so why the heck didn't she?

Her gaze shifted to the files scattered over the bed. Sure,

her job was demanding, and yeah, maybe it was true that she'd become a bit of a workaholic over the years but the truth was she loved it. Gwen poured her heart and soul into her job and over the years she'd become one of the most highly sought-after forensic entomologists in the country. She loved a good mystery, the challenge of solving one, and at the end of the day, there was no greater feeling in the world than helping lock up a killer. Assisting in high-profile investigations made her tick, it was her passion.

Gwen grew up in a small town west of Austin, Texas. Her father was a cop, her mother a teacher. "Little Gwenny," as her mom had called her, was a juxtaposition of an introvert with a fiery hot attitude that put her in more timeouts than she could count. She was always into something, always investigating—taking apart a toy to see how it worked, creating her own recipes and destroying the kitchen in the process, or experimenting with her father's beard trimmers, shaving half her head at age seven. She'd given her parents a run for their money, but they loved her and supported her naturally inquisitive nature in any way they could... while locking up the trimmers, knives, razors, and guns, of course.

From a very early age, Gwen's two favorite things had been collecting bugs and listening to her father talk about working the beat. She was only a freshman in high school when she decided she wanted to be a forensic entomologist. And that was it. Gwen held onto her goal and spent most of her high school years locked away in her room studying, preparing for the career she'd already chosen. And because of that dedication, she graduated valedictorian and received a full-ride to college. She left home at age eighteen, earning a double bachelor's degree in Biology and Chemistry and then received her master's in Entomology.

She'd started her career in forensic entomology assisting local medical examiners, gaining every bit of experience she could while making pennies on the dollar. She approached each job the same, with laser-focus and tireless dedication —regardless of the pay—and quickly earned a name for herself. Nine years and countless seventy-hour workweeks later, Gwen had become an expert in her field, called on frequently by federal agencies to assist in complex homicide investigations. She'd worked her ass off building a reputation for herself and wasn't about to let anything get in the way of that.

Not even a man.

With long, dark hair, big, brown eyes and a tall, lean body, Gwen never had trouble getting a man's attention. Her problem was keeping it. Her job was her number one priority and nothing, not even sex, could bump that out of first place.

It had been six months since her last relationship ended.

I'm sick of having a relationship with your cell phone... Are you ever going to want to settle down... Don't you want to have kids, Ryan had said during their last argument. The kids comment was like a knife in the gut.

She'd met Ryan Melbourne, *esquire*, during one of the cases she'd had to testify on in court. She despised going to court—the suits, formality, the pressure. She preferred to be in the shadows, in the dirt, not in a dress with a microphone in her face, all eyes on her. She didn't even care for lawyers, really, and was surprised at herself when she accepted Ryan's request for a date. But he was handsome, smart, and charismatic, true to the cliché of most lawyers, and she would've been crazy to say no. That first date had stretched into a two-year relationship.

But, no more.

It wasn't just that he'd cheated on her, it wasn't just that she'd invested two years of emotions and energy in something that failed; it was that she blamed herself. Maybe if she had made him a priority. Maybe if she'd taken on fewer cases. Maybe things would have been different.

What was wrong with her?

Her mom told her she should work less... put more focus on her social life. Get married, is what she meant. Gwen refused to put that kind of pressure on herself. It would happen when it was supposed to.

Right?

She laid back on the bed, rested the beer on her navel and blew out a breath.

Beep, beep.

Dammit.

Gwen glanced at the phone and frowned. She recognized the number. It had called at least four times since she'd left the mountain and she was sure some of her unchecked voicemails belonged to it, too.

It was midnight in Oregon, and even later across the country. Pretty damn late to be calling. Repeatedly.

Beep, beep.

She narrowed her eyes, fighting an internal battle. *Dammit, dammit, dammit.*

"Gwyneth Reece here." Work wins again.

"So your phone does work."

Her eyebrows tipped up.

The arrogant caller continued, "You must be a very busy woman, so I'll talk fast."

What the *hell?* Was that annoyance and... *sarcasm* in the man's voice? Who the—

"My name is Wesley Cross, and I'd like to hire you."

She caught a slight southern drawl in the man's deep voice and searched her memory. *Wesley Cross.* She'd never heard the name. No, she didn't know a Wesley Cross and based on the last five seconds, she didn't care to.

"I'm sorry Mr. Cross, I'm not taking any—"

"I'll pay double your fee."

Who the hell was this guy? "As I was *saying,* Mr. Cross—

"Wes."

"Wes. I'm not taking any new cases at this moment."

"Triple. I'll pay triple your fee. I hear you're the best forensic entomologist around and that's what I need."

She sat up, slightly stunned at this odd phone call. "What exactly do you need Mr... Wes?"

"Mr. Wes, I like that. I'll tell you everything when I see you tomorrow morning."

She snorted a laugh. This cocky cowboy was hilarious.

He continued, "I've booked you the five-thirty flight out of PDX, direct flight to Northwest Arkansas and I've reserved a rental car. Full size. Only the best for you."

She could actually hear him smirk on the other end of the phone.

"Wait a second. How do you know where I am?"

"You're working the Caregiver case in the Cascades."

"Stalking is illegal, you know."

"If I were stalking you, you'd know it."

"Four missed calls is stalking."

"Six missed calls, and for someone who works homicides, I'd assume you'd have a better idea of what stalking is."

She narrowed her eyes. "What do you do, Wes?"

"Besides stalking?"

"Besides being a pushy, presumptuous..."

"I hire the best investigators to get me out of a jam. First class, triple your fee. What do you say, Miss Reece?"

"I say you need to get your head checked, Mr. Cross."

"The travel details are in your email. I'll see you tomorrow, Miss Reece. Get some sleep. Sounds like you need it."

"Wait. How did you—

Click.

7

ITH A SMIRK, Wesley tossed his phone on the kitchen counter and picked up his drink. Jessica warned him that Gwyneth Reece ate guys like him for breakfast and based on the short conversation he'd just had with the forensic entomologist, Jessica was right. That was okay though, he never backed away from a challenge. Hell, if he could handle his sister, he could handle any attitude a woman could throw at him.

She'd sounded younger than he'd imagined. Due to her reputation and accolades, he'd assumed she was an older woman with decades of experience under her belt. He'd assumed wrong, and the only thing he knew for certain that she had under her belt was one hell of an attitude.

It hadn't been hard to track her down. He'd had Dean call one of his FBI buddies. Within thirty minutes he'd gotten her email and cell number, and learned she was in Oregon working the Caregiver Killer case; a case that gave even him the chills. Working such a high profile case had been validation that she was exceptional at her job, and made him want her even more.

He took a deep breath and picked up his drink. *Good.* The top entomologist in the country would be in Berry Springs tomorrow morning to help him clear his damn name.

She'd better be, at least.

He knocked back the last remaining sip, poured another two fingers and glanced at the clock—2:03 a.m. It was past midnight in Oregon. He'd been calling Gwyneth all afternoon, getting more and more desperate with each missed call.

After his lunch with Dean and Willard at Donny's Diner, Wesley had busied himself in his shop, getting grease on his hands and blaring good ol' classic rock. He'd needed something to do to keep his mind busy and his thoughts on anything that didn't involve why his ex-lover was brutally murdered in his house. After putting a good dent in his work, he'd dragged himself up to the kitchen, pulled off his sweaty, dirty T-shirt, poured some whiskey and finally, *finally*, had gotten ahold of the attitudinal entomologist.

Feeling a slight bit of relief now, he grabbed his drink, pushed out the back door and stepped onto the deck. It was a dark, moonless night. Not a star in the sky. A cool breeze carrying the scent of rain swept past his bare chest. The storms were coming.

He walked to the edge of the deck, set his drink on the rail, reached into his pocket and pulled out a small bracelet, speckled with blood.

Leena's bracelet. The bracelet he'd won for her at the local fair on their first date.

Wesley ran his fingers over the colorful beads and smiled. Damn thing probably cost three cents to make, but she didn't care. She loved it.

She was wearing it the day she was killed. He'd noticed

it almost immediately, and he wasn't sure why, but he'd taken it off her wrist before the cops showed up. It would've been something else to tie him to her. It was something else that showed how much she really had liked him. It was a stupid move to take it from the crime scene, he knew it, but it was done.

Guilt twisted his stomach.

Why hadn't he given her a chance? If they'd been together, would she still be alive?

He shook his head, dismissing his emotion, and turned the bracelet over in his fingertips. The pool of light from the kitchen window twinkled against the multi-colored beads, and a sparkle of silver caught his eye.

He frowned and peered closer.

Between the beads hung a small, medieval-looking cross pendant with a tiny green gemstone in the center. The edges were worn, the intricate carving faded.

What the hell?

He was certain the pendant hadn't been on the bracelet when he'd given it to Leena. He was sure because she'd showed him the beads closely, remarking that they reminded her of one of her grandmother's dresses. He'd gotten a good look then, and no, a creepy-ass-looking cross definitely was not on the bracelet.

Where did it come from?

Thunder rumbled in the distance.

He held the small pendant between his fingers and looked closer, noticing it had been added with a thin string, loosely tied onto the hemp. Like someone had haphazardly done it.

Like someone was in a hurry.

≈

"...expected landing time five minutes. Thank you for flying with us today, and welcome to Northwest Arkansas, y'all."

Gwen jerked awake at the sound of the flight attendant's sugary-sweet voice coming through the speaker. She blinked, sat up and checked her watch, which had automatically adjusted to the two-hour time change—9:03 a.m. She stretched her neck and looked around.

First class wasn't bad at all. Not bad *at all*.

Of all the times she'd traveled, she'd never sprung for first class. Blame it on her humble upbringing. But after this morning, she'd have to rethink that. Usually unable to sleep on planes, Gwen had fallen fast asleep within fifteen minutes of takeoff and slept like a rock.

She lifted the shade and looked out the rain-streaked window.

Rain?

When did that start?

She peered down at the colorful mountains below— muted colors of orange, red and yellow, like splattered paint against soaring peaks. Even with the dim overcast, it was beautiful. It reminded her of home, and a warm feeling swept over her.

She felt surprisingly alert and refreshed. Ready to take on the day, which was a nice change from how she'd felt the last few days.

After she'd hung up with the cocky Wesley Cross the evening before, her curiosity had gotten the best of her, and after grabbing another beer, she settled in to research Berry Springs. The small, country town was only an eight-hour drive from her home in Texas, which meant she could escape at any time and head home if she needed to, without having to wait on a flight. And that was what sealed the deal.

Well, that *and* triple her fee. *Triple!*

Another beer after that, she'd decided she was going to inflate her fee. Payback for Mr. Cross's relentless pestering. And after her fourth beer, she'd decided she was going to take a three-day vacation to Hawaii after the little adventure. And with that exciting thought, she'd fallen asleep with visions of muscled-up beach boys and Mai Tai's in her head.

As the plane descended, she found herself wondering what Wesley looked like, as she had done a hundred times since they'd hung up. His voice was deep, smooth, and that southern drawl was pretty damn sexy, she had to admit. But it was his confidence that intrigued her the most. In their short three-minute conversation, Gwen knew Wesley was the type of guy that didn't take no for an answer, and she got the vibe he didn't hear it much in the first place.

The plane skidded to a stop on a bumpy runway surrounded by cow pastures. A surprisingly short twenty-minutes later she was through the teeny-tiny airport and in her rental car. Full size, just as he promised. A nice, roomy Tahoe. Not bad at all.

Despite the thick cloud cover, it was a mild sixty-three degrees. Typical fall weather for the area. She plugged in the address Wesley had texted her early this morning. No *sorry for hounding you last night*, or, *have you made a decision*, or, *sorry to text so early*, just the address and the words *Ask for Jessica*. He just assumed she'd accepted his offer and because of that, she didn't bother to respond. She just packed up and headed to the airport.

Make him sweat a bit.

As she exited the airport, the dark clouds above opened up, and a deluge rained down on her. She sighed and prayed this wasn't a sign of things to come. After turning the windshield wipers on high, Gwen began her journey through the narrow, mountain roads. As she drove deeper into the valleys, she was awestruck at the nature that surrounded her. Jagged cliffs hugged one side of the road, steep ravines, the other. In a few spots, she had to slow down due to the water rushing over the road. Beautiful, yes, but not an easy drive, especially on roads that she wasn't familiar with.

She fumbled with the radio and landed on a national news channel.

"... *rains pounding the South. Heavy thunderstorms and flash flooding is going to be a major concern over the next few days. Now onto the biggest story of the day. After two long months, the serial killer haunting the Northwest, known as the Caregiver Killer...*"

Her eyes widened, her back straightened like a rod.

"... *has finally been caught thanks to forensic evidence found at the scene yesterday afternoon linking the latest victim to a local sewage plant, where the suspect was employed. Authorities found the body of another elderly woman hidden in a bunker at the plant. The suspect's name is not being released at this time. Our own Drew Simmons is live at the scene...*"

Gwen's jaw dropped. They finally found him. The Caregiver Killer had been caught... thanks to *her*. Goosebumps ran over her arms and tears stung her eyes. The families of the victims could finally begin the process of healing. No more wondering, no more fear. No more living with the unknown.

She took a shaky breath, overcome with emotions. *This* is why she did what she did. *This* made every sleepless night she had buried in work, every lonely night without a man, and all the endless hours spent in airports totally and completely worth it.

She fought the urge to call Agent Stein, knowing he was busier than ever with the latest development.

Feeling a bit lighter now, she turned on some classic

rock and focused on the wet road ahead until she passed the sign that read *Welcome to Berry Springs*. Her attention shifted to two young teenagers on horseback galloping along the side of the road—in the pouring rain. Both wore cowboy hats—with water pouring off the sides—shiny belt buckles and smiles the size of Texas. She smirked, knowing they were having the time of their lives. She drove past a discount grocery store, snickering at the people darting to their cars with paper sacks over their heads. Then, there was the county sale barn. Apparently, it was sale day. She'd never seen so many pickup trucks, trailers, and apprehensive cows in one place. She passed a few signs for hiking trails and horseback riding adventures and for a second, actually considered checking it out. During her research, she'd learned that Berry Springs was a big tourist location, attracting people from all over the country for hiking, camping and boating on Otter Lake. Before she could blink, she was passing through town square which appeared to be the hub of the small town. The storefronts were thoughtfully decorated with fall décor, mainly hay bales and pots of colorful mums. She spotted a few *Happy Fall, Y'all* signs. American flags hung from the antique light posts that lined the two-lane road. Despite the weather, the square buzzed with activity, with people going in and out of Fanny's Farm and Feed and Tad's Tool shop. The busiest spot was a restaurant named Donny's Diner.

Her mouth watered as she drove by. Something about the blue-checked curtains and bright red booths in the windows made her want to pull in for a warm piece of apple pie and coffee.

But she had an appointment to get to.

According to Google Maps, she was one minute away from her destination. She slid under a yellow light, clicked on her turn signal and parked underneath a soaring oak tree next to a metal sign that read *County Coroner.*

The morgue.

The inconspicuous building looked like an innocent medical clinic, but healing sick people was not what went on behind the closed doors.

Gwen had seen countless dead bodies, but usually at crime scenes where she was able to put the gore aside and focus on the job at hand. The morgue was different. Something about multiple corpses just hanging out in freezers gave her the willies. The bodies would eventually be buried, burned, or get sliced into and examined in a hundred different ways. Organs laid on tables, next to tools that looked to be straight out of a torture chamber. It made her sick to her stomach. Crime scenes were organic, at least. Horrific or not, they were organic. Bodies getting sliced open on silver tables was not.

The pounding rain against the roof buzzed like a million bugs and she kicked herself for not packing an umbrella. She took note of a white van parked across the street, with the running lights on. A media van?

Humph.

A media van outside the morgue meant at least one body inside was high profile and for the first time since last night, she wondered what the heck she was doing. Why had she accepted a job she knew nothing about—not a single damn thing. She hated not being prepared and felt like a fish out of water.

Gwen closed her eyes and momentarily disappeared to Hawaii, thanks to her tripled fee.

Yes, a little sun, sandy beach, crystal-blue waves washing against her freshly done pedicure.

Ahhhhhh.

With that uplifting thought, Gwen pulled down the visor and flicked up the mirror. Unlike most jobs, wearing suits and heels wasn't a requirement for analyzing bugs simply because they didn't care what she looked like. But because she was going into this particular job blind, she'd decided to slap on some makeup—courtesy of the free samples she'd gotten with an eye-boggling expensive anti-aging serum she'd recently purchased. So far, the serum hadn't done a thing on its long list of promises, but the makeup stayed true to its long-lasting guarantee.

Good job, samples, she thought and made a mental note to stick with the brand.

Her hair was another story. Thanks to the one-hundred percent humidity, her long brown hair had curled at the ends and frizzed at the top. She ran her fingers through it, which only puffed it out more, so she tied it back into a ponytail. She smoothed her white sweater, which she'd paired with dark skinny jeans and boots.

With a quick inhale, she grabbed her purse and brief-case and darted up the sidewalk, jumping under the measly three-inch overhang just above the door. Rain ran like a waterfall over the gutters. She pressed her body up against the door and tried the handle—locked.

The rain splattered against her boots as she knocked—nothing.

She banged her fist against the door.

"No solicitations." A gruff, female voice crackled through a speaker just below the ancient-looking doorbell that she hadn't even noticed.

Gwen leaned into the speaker and pressed the silver button where the paint had worn off from so many fingers touching it—apparently trying to get past the guard dog inside. "My name is Gwyneth Reece. I was told you'd be expecting me," she said quickly, with a hint of impatience.

Silence.

Finally, a *click*, and the door swung open. "Ah, it's raining." Dressed in a white lab coat, a short, stocky redhead stepped back, motioning her inside. Gwen noticed the bevy of tattoos on her wrist as she held the door open.

Gwen wiped her boots on the *Go Away* mat as the guard dog sent a *screw-you* scowl toward the media van before closing the door. Intimidating by all counts, especially for her small frame.

"Sorry, I thought—"

"I was a solicitor. Yeah, I heard."

The green-eyed redhead smirked, then said, "Believe it or not, we get 'em. Most people avoid morgues like the plague, but not solicitors... or journalists for that matter." The disdain for the profession evident in her voice. "Especially when there's a dead body found in town. They're like goddamned gnats you can't get rid of. No offense."

Gwen laughed and decided she liked whoever this southern firecracker was. "None taken."

"I'm Jessica Heathrow." She smiled. "The medical examiner."

They shook hands and Gwen couldn't help but notice how young she looked. Younger than any other medical examiner she'd met.

"Gwyneth Reece." She took a quick glance around the small, front office, noticing the overhead lights were off. A clock on the wall ticked loudly against the silence.

"I've heard a lot about you. Even watched one of the presentations you gave at Stanford, I believe."

"Ah, I hope it was a nice nap."

Jessica laughed boisterously.

"So, to be honest, I have no idea why I'm here."

"Follow me."

Gwen followed the ME through a metal door and into the laboratory that took up the rest of the building. It was a large space with four silver tables surrounded by lights and trays of tools from hell. Six freezers stretched across the back wall, and a desk with multiple computer screens sat in the corner. Along the far side, a long counter with a sink, cabinets, microscopes, beakers and everything else you'd expect to see in a lab.

The room was dark except for a single light in the back corner, illuminating a table covered with a gray sheet draped over a body. Blonde hair spilled over the side.

"Sorry about the lack of lights. Thought maybe the news gnats would head home."

"News gnats. I might use that name in the future."

"You should quote me in one of your presentations. You know, as the sexy, smart, *single* medical examiner."

Gwen laughed. "The only thing you'd want less than media vans outside your doors are a bunch of male entomologists. Trust me."

"Hey if there's one thing I've learned about analyzing the dead is that you need to date someone with a similar profession."

"I heard that," Gwen muttered.

As expected, she was being led straight to the sheet.

"I can't believe you're here, really. Although knowing Wesley..." Jessica's voice trailed off.

"Knowing Wesley, what?"

"Doesn't take 'no' too kindly. If there's a challenge, he's like a dog with a bone." She glanced over her shoulder, giving Gwen the once-over. "You met him yet?"

"Not yet."

A slight grin crossed the ME's lips before she looked away.

A grin? What was that about? *Dammit,* she hated being out of the loop.

Hawaii, Hawaii, Hawaii, she repeated in her head.

They walked up to the table and without preamble, Jessica yanked back the gray sheet. "She's why you're here."

Gwen's stomach rolled as she looked down at the open wound gaping from the young woman's throat. She could see all the way to the bone. The blood had been drained from the woman's body, leaving bluish-gray skin. It was like staring down at a wax figure in a horror flick.

"Who is she?"

"Leena Ross, age thirty-three. Kidnapped, although that's assumed, throat slashed, left to bleed to death."

"Time of death?"

"About midnight Thursday night, technically Friday morning. Close to. She's been dead around thirty hours, estimated."

"Where was she found? Inside or outside?"

Jessica paused, and Gwen noticed. "Inside. A basement."

"Struggle?"

"Kind of." Jessica peeled back the sheet and pointed to the knife mark on Leena's side, that indicated she'd been forced into a car at knifepoint. She then showed her the bruising on Leena's arms indicating the killer pinned her down from behind to slice her throat.

Gwen shook her head. Young, blonde, beautiful. Wasted life.

"Suspect?"

"Nope."

"What about her folks? Did they have anything useful?"

"No... no one seems to have any idea who would do this to her."

"Okay. How can I help?"

"I found insect eggs in her wound."

Gwen blinked. No way in hell was that why she was flown across the country. She cleared her throat. "Uh, that's not uncommon."

"It is for only being dead a few minutes, at the most, before she was found. And for being killed inside a building."

"Only a few minutes before someone found her?"

"Yep. And she wasn't left alone after that. Authorities were on the scene almost immediately. They wouldn't let bugs trample over her."

"Okay, I see. Yes, this would be uncommon, then."

Jessica yanked a pair of latex gloves from a box on the silver rolling table and handed them to her. "I was surprised, to say the least. Didn't add up."

"You're sure she was murdered inside? A home, or what?"

Jessica glanced away for a quick second. "Yes. I'm sure, and yes, a home."

Gwen watched her for a moment. Jessica wasn't telling her something.

"You're sure they're insect eggs? Eggs at all, even?" She slid on the gloves.

"One-hundred percent. I'd say at least half of my bodies come in with maggots. I'm very familiar."

"And they were *in* the wound?"

"Almost two inches in."

Humph. Yes, this *was* interesting. Something wasn't adding up.

Jessica continued, "I took samples of the eggs, storing

some in alcohol and some in vials over there. They've just hatched."

Gwen frowned in deep thought. "If they've just hatched, the eggs were fresh."

Jessica shrugged. "Not sure; that's your area. I checked again just a few hours ago, and some are still unhatched."

Good. That was good.

"We're obviously hoping you can uncover something to help lead us to whoever did this. My only disturbance to the laceration was removing the eggs to confirm they were indeed eggs. Samples are on the counter, over there." She motioned toward the far side of the room. "Probably not the most high-tech equipment you're used to, but not bad for little ol' Berry Springs."

"It will work just fine, thanks. Do you have the case file?"

"Oh. Yes, thanks, almost forgot." Jessica yanked a folder from the counter. "Here you go. Not much there, I'm 'fraid, considering it's a fresh case. Probably not as thorough as you'd like but it has all the necessary details and initial analysis." A phone rang from the office up front. "Gotta get that. I'll leave you alone. Oh, here's a lab coat and glasses."

"Perfect, thanks."

"You need a coffee, water...?"

"No, thanks."

"Okay, *mi casa, su casa*. Use whatever you need. Holler if you need anything."

"Thanks."

Gwen slipped the lab coat over her clothes as Jessica's footsteps faded. The white coat was about four sizes too big and the glasses—more like goggles—were, too.

She turned back to the body. Now she knew why she was there, but the only thing she didn't understand is what Wesley Cross had to do with it. He said he wanted to hire her to "*get him out of a jam.*" He had to be involved somehow. Related to the victim, maybe?

She opened up her briefcase and got to work.

Minutes ticked into hours as she worked tunnel-visioned in the silence until a boom of thunder pulled her from her focus. She straightened and glanced at the clock—1:33 p.m. She'd been working for over three hours already. As if on cue, her stomach growled. She took a deep breath, stretched her neck from side-to-side and yanked off her gloves. Maybe a quick break to check email and snack on the protein bar she'd tossed in her purse. And a coffee... a coffee sounded great.

Gwen turned and startled at the dark silhouette of a man standing in the doorway across the room, staring at her.

"*Good Lord,* you scared me."

The first thing she noticed was the sheer mass of the silhouette. Tall and thick as a bull. He stood motionless, in a way that made her want to check over her shoulder to make sure one of the bodies hadn't jumped out of the freezer.

She swallowed the knot in her throat, squinted and cocked her head.

"Sorry," the man said.

She recognized the smooth, deep voice instantly. Wesley Cross.

As he crossed the dark lab, the fluorescent light above her slowly illuminated his face.

And butterflies tickled her stomach.

8

*W*ESLEY CROSS WAS *hot*. Like, ruggedly handsome, drop-to-your-knees, *gorgeous*. He reminded her of a sexy cowboy from the early westerns, the black and whites where the men rode horseback, smoked cigars, and the hard look in their eyes dared you to disrespect them. As he drew closer she decided, no, he wouldn't be the cowboy... he'd be the bank robber with that cocky grin and a twinkle in his eye. The kind of guy that could get away with anything.

His gaze pinned her as he crossed the room, blurring everything and everyone around it.

She glanced down and shifted her weight, and—*Oh, God*—the oversized lab coat and enormous goggles. Of all the times to look like the damn Michelin Man. Gwen quickly slid the glasses to the top of her head and squared her shoulders with an attempt to come off as confident, despite the unbalance she suddenly felt.

"You must be Gwyneth." The fresh scent of rain accompanied him as he walked up. He wore a black T-shirt with the words *Cross Combat* across the chest, faded jeans and cowboy boots. His hair was wet with speckles of gray at the temples that had her wondering how much older he was than her.

His gaze skimmed her body, and her stomach fluttered in response. She felt like she was back in junior high and the star quarterback had just taken notice of her. This was ridiculous. *She* was being ridiculous.

She thrust out her hand. "Yes. Gwyneth Reece."

He smiled, widely, as if laughing at her professionalism. They shook hands, a firm shake against skin that was no stranger to manual labor.

"Wesley Cross. Call me Wes."

"Okay." She glanced over his shoulder.

"She ran to get something to eat." He said, reading her thoughts.

Another boom of thunder, and this time, the windows shook.

"Hope she has an umbrella."

"Supposed to rain for two days straight." He paused, his gaze sweeping over her lips, then slowly trailing back up to her eyes. "You're different than I expected."

"You were expecting beady, black eyes and antennas poking out of my head?"

He laughed. It was a nice laugh. Deep. Sexy. She wanted to ask what he meant exactly—was she younger, older, taller, or worst-case scenario, not as attractive as he'd expected—but decided to stay on task. Focus on the job at hand.

"Well," she opened up her palms. "You got me. Here I am."

He looked past her at the blonde on the table, the twinkle in his blue eyes disappearing. "Thank you for coming. Really."

Gwen nodded and turned toward the table. "I've been here since around ten. I have some questions—"

"What have you found so far?"

"I'd like to get a better understanding of the scene before reporting my findings."

Something flickered in his eyes. "Just tell me what you've found so far."

"No." The defiance strong in her voice. "Not until I get some questions answered."

He stared at her for a moment. "Hungry?"

Her eyebrow arched at the abrupt and seemingly inappropriate change of subject. "No. I mean, well, yes. I've got a protein bar in my bag that I was just about to eat."

"Manufactured protein is overrated."

"Oh, well, your opinion means everything to me, Mr. Cross."

"It was Mr. Wes last night." He smirked. "Seriously. Protein bars taste like cardboard. How about some real food?"

Real food sounded like heaven, and it would be a good opportunity to gain some more insight into the case. Before she could formally accept, he smiled and said, "Good. Let's go."

"We should wait for Jessica to get back."

"I'll lock it from the inside. She'll be back soon."

"Okay, well," Gwen looked down at the circus tent that draped her. "Let me just..." She slipped it off, covered Leena's body with the sheet, and grabbed her purse. "Alright."

As he led her out of the lab, her eyes drifted to his backside, powerless to not take a look at the way his jeans hugged his ass.

He paused at the front door, scanning the coat rack. "No umbrella."

"Didn't take you for an umbrella kind of guy. No offense."

"Definitely none taken there. I was looking for you." He glanced at the rain pounding the sidewalk. "Stay here. Come out when I pull up."

"No, it's fine. My boots are already soaked. I don't mind getting wet."

The corner of his lip curled up as her last statement lingered in the air. "Be right back."

She watched him jog to his truck, the wet T-shirt melting across his shoulders. Wesley Cross was built like an ox.

Gwen slowly shook her head from side-to-side and muttered, "Un-*believable.*" Of all the things she'd expected to happen in Berry Springs, meeting a man that gave her butterflies wasn't one of them.

A second later, a brand-new, blacked-out truck zoomed up from the side, hopped the sidewalk, and skidded to a stop inches from the front door. Instinctively, she jumped back from the window. She looked at the media van—were they seeing this?

Wesley got out and opened the passenger side door. After taking two spidey-like leaps over puddles, and jumped into his truck. After locking the office door, he slid behind the wheel.

"You didn't have to do that." She said.

"Of course I did. If I had an overcoat, I would've laid it over the puddles for you." He looked at her and winked as he pulled out of the parking lot.

"Like the black and whites, huh? The good ol' days."

"Like a good, southern gentleman."

"Those still around?"

He slid her a glance. "Absolutely... And challenge accepted, Miss Reece."

She smiled at the twinkle in his eye as he said it. "Do you consider stalking a woman and not taking no for an answer a characteristic of a gentleman?"

"I do." He said matter-of-factly.

"Well, so do eighty-percent of people in prison."

He laughed. "You're a tough gal to get ahold of."

"You almost ran my battery out."

"Time is of the essence."

"And the *why* is exactly what I want to learn at lunch."

"Jessica explained everything to you, right?"

"The Cliffs Notes version. There's more to this story, and I want to know it." When he didn't respond, she said, "A gentleman never keeps a lady in the dark."

A devilish smirk crossed his face. "Only if the occasion calls for it."

Just then, lightning sparked ahead of them. She leaned forward and looked at the sky, and something tumbled down her back. *The goggles.* She'd forgotten to take them off. Her eyes rounded and her mouth dropped. Seething, she looked at Wesley, who was chuckling.

"Something wrong?" He asked, grinning.

"Oh, no, not at all." The annoyance and sarcasm dripping from her voice. "I just *love* wearing autopsy goggles around town. *Geez, Wesley*, these could have human... fluids or something on them. Why didn't you tell me?"

"Wes. And I thought you looked cute in them. Lab teacher hot."

"So cliché." She stuffed them into her purse as a crack of thunder had her nerves jumping out of her skin, followed by another flash of lightning.

"You ever been here?" He asked.

"To Berry Springs? No."

"We get wild weather at the change of the seasons. Supposed to get quite a bit of flooding with this storm."

"Too bad you didn't reserve me a rental boat, then."

"I have one of my own I could lend you. Anyway, I figured you'd be used to seasonal storms. Not too different from your hometown."

"No, not too different at all." She blinked. He knew where she lived. She turned to him with narrowed eyes. "*Alright*, I don't know who you had dig into me, or how exactly you knew I was on a job in Oregon. Or, how you got my personal cell phone number, but I'm feeling like a fish out of water here, and that's going to change right now. For starters, what do you do, Wes?"

He was smiling ear-to-ear, entertained at the attitude in her voice. He flicked on his turn signal and slid into the only open parking spot on the town square. The sign above an aged, red wooden door read *Gino's Pizzeria.*

"We're here." He turned off the truck, pulled the keys from the ignition and looked at her. "To answer your question, I make guns for a living. Now can you relax a little so we can eat?"

Before she could respond, he was out of the truck and at her window.

He opened her door, the rain pouring down his face. "A gentleman." He smiled and winked.

God, what had she gotten herself into?

Wesley held open the door for Gwen, taking a moment to check out her curves as she breezed past him—with just a touch of attitude in the sway of her hips. Her *sexy* hips. The woman was nothing like he'd imagined and her sarcastic description wasn't too far off—beady eyes and antennas. Truth was, he didn't expect anyone who studied flesh-eating bugs for a living to be attractive, let alone smoking hot.

But she was. Gwyneth Reece was smoking hot and *all woman*.

When he'd walked into the lab, the first thing he'd noticed was the long, brown ponytail that cascaded down her back. Pretty, silky hair was his first surprise.

His second surprise was when she'd turned around, and behind the God-awful goggles, were the most beautiful deep brown eyes he'd ever seen in his life. Like chocolate. Smooth, milk chocolate above a pair of lips just as mouth-watering—big, pouty, and rosy pink.

The third and biggest surprise was the little kick his heart gave when their eyes met.

One thing Wesley prided himself on was that he was rarely thrown off his game. Rarely surprised. But when the snippy, impatient entomologist from the phone call the night before turned around in that lab, he was *floored* by her beauty.

The invite to lunch was two-fold—he'd never been in the vicinity of a beautiful woman and not asked her out and, based on the attitude she'd given him when he asked for information, he knew he needed to loosen her up a bit. At least before he told her that the body she'd been working on all morning was found in *his* basement. He'd made Jessica promise not to say anything in case it scared her off. Would she instantly think the guy who'd talked her into helping him out was the killer?

He stepped next to her as the owner-slash-waiter-slash-cook, Gus Dickey, called out from the kitchen. "Howdy, Wesley! Sit where you'd like."

The small Italian restaurant was quiet, with only two people sitting at the bar. The dim lights, dark hardwood floors, and antique jukebox gave a subtle romantic vibe, although he hadn't thought about that when he'd chosen the restaurant. The only other option close was Donny's which would be packed for lunch, and he didn't want to deal with the whispers and side-long glances implying his involvement in Leena's death. He didn't want Gwen to notice, either.

Wesley motioned to the seats. "You pick."

Gwen led him to the back corner booth. Exactly where he would've chosen. He slid in across from her as she looked over the menu, wasting no time. Very hungry, apparently.

"Try the pizza. Best around."

She shrugged, keeping her gaze on the menu.

"You'll regret it if you don't. Trust me."

Gus walked up, wiping his tanned, calloused hands on an apron that said *kiss the cook*. His hair was freshly buzzed, highlighting the deep scar above his right ear. To this day, Wesley didn't know if Gus chose buzzers because the style was low maintenance, or to showcase the scar like a badge of honor. The former Green Beret had opened the restaurant years earlier and due to their similar backgrounds, Gus and Wesley had become instant friends, spending many late nights at the bar discussing the thin line between war and peace. Wesley had yet to pay for a single beer.

"Howdy do, Cross?" Gus's curious gaze flickered to Gwen. "Ma'am."

She nodded, flashing a polite smile, and both men smiled back. Hard not to smile back at that face.

"What can I get ya?"

Wesley nodded to Gwen for her to go first.

"Iced tea, please. Unsweet."

"You got it." He turned to Wesley.

"Shiner, please."

"Be right back to take your orders."

Gwen finally set down the menu and focused on him with a pensive look. Inquisitive. Or was it skepticism? Doubt? He stared back and knew instantly that those whiskey brown eyes didn't miss much. Those lips pressed into a thin line, and he braced himself for the onslaught of questions that were about to barrel out of her.

"Tell me about what happened. I want to know everything about Leena Ross."

"And then you'll tell me what you found today?"

"Yes."

Wesley glanced at Gus behind the bar, wanting at least one sip of booze in his system before diving into the story. He looked back at Gwen, the sudden intensity of her gaze blinding like a spotlight. Damn, the woman was... a lot.

He cleared his throat. "Leena and I had been... friendly a few months ago..."

"Friendly, as in intimate?"

No, those brown eyes didn't miss much. "That's right."

Gwen nodded as if the news didn't surprise her and a moment of insecurity shot through him. What the hell was it about him that screamed womanizer?

"We went on a few dates here and there and that was it."

"Here you guys go." Gus slid their drinks onto the table. "Ready to order?"

Wesley took two huge gulps of beer as Gwen ordered an Italian chicken salad.

"Medium meat trio, double cheese," he ordered when she was done.

"You got it." Gus walked away.

Wesley took one more sip, then continued. "Night before last, technically yesterday, I came home and found her in my basement."

Her eyes rounded. "In your *home*?"

He nodded.

She blinked for a moment, processing the information. "Wait... so your ex-girlfriend was murdered—her throat brutally slashed—in your home?"

"Literally, minutes before I got there. Best we can tell she was kidnapped from her apartment."

"Was anyone else there?"

"No. I live alone."

"Did you see anyone?"

He nodded. "From a distance. And I chased him into the woods. It was dark. Son of a bitch—'scuse the language—jumped into an SUV and drove off. Didn't see his face, couldn't even tell the make or model of the vehicle. Nothing."

"Did anyone see anyone? Neighbors, whatever?"

"No. I live off the radar; in the woods."

She stared at him for a moment, the stun apparent and unsurprising.

"Jessica said there's no suspects, is that right?"

He shifted in his seat. "Not that I'm aware of. Not right now."

"Besides you, right?" Blunt and to-the-point. He had to respect that.

"I have a dozen alibis for when it happened."

A heavy second ticked by.

"Was anything found at the scene?"

He paused for a second, considering the bracelet, then decided to keep that close. For now. "No. The basement door was broken into. Latex powder found on the knob."

"He wore gloves."

"Right. Tire tracks were faded with mine, so that gives us jack-shit."

Gwen mindlessly stirred her tea in deep thought. "Your former lover, taken to your house and murdered while you were gone..."

"Thanks for the recap."

"A setup is the obvious angle here, right?"

"Right."

"So you need to clear your name."

"It's not just that..."

"No, it's not." Her eyes leveled on his. "You think there's more to this than a setup."

"I do."

She nodded, less skepticism now. "Okay. Now I see why you were so desperate to get me over here."

He leaned back, relieved. At least the woman wasn't walking out the door.

"The *only* thing they've found that seems odd, or *off*, is the eggs in her wound. So, after hearing you were the best forensic entomologist around, I called you up."

"Stalked me."

He grinned, sipped.

"Okay, now I feel less like a fish out of water about the case, but there's still something you and I need to clear up. How did you know where I was? *And* get my personal phone number and email?"

"A buddy has an FBI buddy."

She shot him a look laced with disapproval just as Gus delivered their food. Her salad was limp and boring, his pizza—glorious. He caught her eyeing the steaming pie. He tore a piece away, put it on a napkin, and slid it across the table. "Try it. You have to."

She grabbed her fork and shook her head. "I'm good."

"You can't come to Gino's and not try the pizza."

"Man, you are one persistent..."

He winked.

"For the sake of avoiding another battle..." Gwen picked up the slice and bit in. Her eyes sparkled as she chewed.

A wave of pleasure swept over him. "Eh? Good, huh?"

"As much as I hate to admit it, yeah. Yeah, it's incredible."

"Hey, Gus! Need another plate over here."

Gus laughed as he set a plate on the table. "Can't come here and not try my pie."

Gwen nodded. "Pretty darn good."

Wesley loaded the plate with the cheesiest pieces and slid it in front of her. She picked at her salad, pretending to enjoy it—because God forbid that he'd been right—before taking another bite of pizza. He tried to hide his smile, watching her. He liked her. She was funny. Not in an obvious way, but funny to him, nonetheless.

He let her focus on devouring her pizza as he finished his own. After he was sure she was satisfied, he returned to the conversation at hand.

"Okay, now you know the background of why you're here. Now, will you tell me what you've found? It's weird, right? The eggs?"

Gwen washed down the last bite with a gulp of tea, looked at him and nodded. "Yes, it's weird." She took a deep breath. "Okay, flies lay eggs in moist places like the eyes or the mouth..."

"Or a wound."

"Right, but the first thing I noticed is that there were no eggs anywhere else on her body. Not the eyes, mouth, nowhere. This is a bit odd, but not enough to necessarily raise any flags. The second thing I noticed was that the eggs were scattered throughout the laceration in her neck, from the initial piercing and all the way across. I even found some on the other side. Only a few eggs, here and there. Very, *very* easy to miss without a trained eye. Now, *this* was odd."

"Odd that the eggs were spread across the wound?"

"Right."

"How so?"

"Flies lay anywhere from seventy-five to a hundred-and-fifty eggs at a time—

"And there weren't that many."

She held up a finger in a way that give him instant hot-teacher fantasies.

"Hang on, I'm not finished. As I was saying, they lay around a hundred at a time, in clumps. *Clumps* of eggs. As I said, the eggs found in Leena's throat were scattered; a few here and there, across the gash. This definitely is not typical."

"Are you saying the wound was tampered with after the fact? After she was killed?"

"Not if the story you've told me is correct. Not if your timeline is correct. Is it correct?"

"Yes."

"You said that you got there just minutes after it happened, right? And the killer had already hightailed it out, right?"

"Right."

"So then, in that short amount of time, there's no way a fly would've found the body, landed, nested, and laid eggs. And even if it did, there definitely wouldn't have been time to allow whoever to dive back into the wound and smear the eggs around."

Wesley nodded. She was right... and she wasn't finished. He stared at her, hanging on her every word as she leaned forward, her eyes flashing with intensity.

In a low voice, she finally said, "Wes, what I'm saying is... the insect eggs that were found in Leena's throat were transferred directly from the murder weapon."

9

*W*ESLEY BURST THROUGH the lab door with Gwen hot on his heels.

Hovered over Leena's autopsy table, Jessica straightened and turned, wide-eyed at the sudden eruption in her once-silent laboratory.

"How far have you gotten examining the laceration?" He strode up to the table.

Jessica cast a confused glance at Gwen, then focused back on Wesley. "'Bout finished up my end of it. Gwen will close the loop regarding the eggs. What the hell's going on here?"

"Gwen thinks the eggs were transferred from the murder weapon."

Jessica's mouth gaped. "*What?*"

He listened to Gwen tell her theory to Jessica, his mind racing a million miles a minute. As soon as she finished, he asked, "Have you confirmed what kind of knife was used to cut her throat?"

"Yes. Six-inch serrated blade."

A tingle shot up his spine. "A hunting knife."

Jessica's eyes were still wide from this new development. "It's a strong possibility." She looked at Gwen. "Hell of a lead, Gwen."

Gwen gave a quick nod, and then her face hardened again. "*If* it were a hunting knife, it would've had to have been in contact with a rotting carcass right before the incident. Like, *right* before."

"Which challenges the theory that it was well thought out."

"Not necessarily." Wesley began pacing. "The obvious is a hunter, right?"

"Hunting season just started up, too," Jessica added.

He ran his fingers through his wet hair. "Who else? What other scenarios would have a knife around maggots?"

Gwen chewed on her lower lip. "Trash... a garbage truck."

"Yes. And anywhere there's rotting meat." Jessica nodded enthusiastically. "And what about taxidermy?"

Wesley nodded. "Yes. We need to look at all these people in the area." His eyes darted around the room. "We need to write this down."

Jessica grabbed a sticky note and began taking notes.

"What about dog shit... like kennels?" Wesley asked. The fresh rush of adrenaline had him talking fast, and trying to mask the hint of desperation in his voice. Desperate looked good on no man.

"Good thinking; maggots can be found in animal feces," Gwen said. "We should also check meat vendors at the farmer's market. Local farmers who skin and cut their own meat."

"Good idea." Wesley pulled out his phone. "Okay, so, we'll hit the sanitation department, area landfills, taxidermist, dog kennels, farmer's market vendors..."

"And talk to your sister about the gun range," Jessica added. "Has anyone come in bragging about their kills this season? Maybe purchasing a new knife?"

"Good... yes." Still pacing, he rubbed his jaw. While Gwen and Jessica were building a list, he started going down a different path. He turned to Jessica. "We need to test the wound for any blood that isn't Leena's." He looked at Gwen, seeking reassurance for what he was about to say. "If insect eggs were on the knife, the eggs had to have been transferred with something sticky to stick to the knife, right? Blood, probably?"

Gwen nodded. "That's right. Any kind of bodily fluid."

"Whether from a human or an animal, right?"

She nodded.

"Wait a second, guys." Jessica shook her head. "Do you understand how much blood spilled from her neck? How much of *her* blood? The odds of it washing away *any* kind of fluid..."

"We have to check, Jess."

"I mean..." Jessica glanced down at Leena's lifeless body on the table, and paused, her face squeezing in deep thought. "Maybe..." she muttered. "Maybe if I check where the blade initially pierced the skin. The likelihood of a transfer of any kind would be greatest there."

Gwen stepped forward. "And the outer folds of skin. The outside of the laceration where any substance would have made first contact with the skin."

Jessica's head bobbed up and down. "Yes, yes."

"Assuming you find blood that isn't Leena's..." Wesley paused to gather his thoughts. He felt hyped up like he had a runner's high. *Finally, something.*

"It's a big assumption, Wesley. I don't want you to get your hopes up."

He cast Jessica an icy look. "Assuming you do, we've got two scenarios. Human DNA or animal. Human would be the holy grail here because the odds of it being the killer's is huge. And if it were animal, it would at least help narrow down who we're looking for. It would confirm we're looking in the right place, too."

Pity crossed Jessica's eyes. "You're reaching."

"It's *something*, Jess," he snapped and turned away.

Uncomfortable with the mounting tension, Gwen stepped between him and Jessica. "I want to examine the eggs that have just hatched and take another look at the wound before I write up my final report and head to the airport."

Wesley stopped on a dime and looked over his shoulder at Gwen. *Head to the airport.* She was leaving. Already. She met his gaze with a look he couldn't quite read, then looked away. His gut twisted. He didn't want her to leave, but as quickly as that unsettling thought materialized, he pushed it aside. Spending more time with the incredibly sexy entomologist was not what he needed to focus on.

Wesley turned to Jessica. "How long to check the blood?"

"Give me a day, at least. Twenty-four hours. I'll jump right on it, you know that, but she's not the only body I'm working on." Jessica looked at Gwen. "I'll get out of your way until you finish. I've got some reports to catch up on in the office." She glanced at Wesley before leaving the room. "I'll call you as soon as I know anything new."

"Thanks, Jess."

He watched Jessica leave, feeling Gwen's eyes on him.

"I'm sorry I can't be of more help," she said.

He snorted. "Seriously? Gwen, before you, we had absolutely nothing. Now we have a pool of people to look at; a narrowed down list. You've given us our first lead. A good one."

She smiled a soft smile and held his gaze for a moment, then cleared her throat and looked away. "I'll leave my report with Jessica when I leave."

"Wait." Like a magnet being pulled, he closed the inches between them. "Gwen. Can I..."

The front door opened and overlapping chatter from the office ensued. Dean and Willard pushed through the lab doors.

"Hey, Wesley." Dean's attention shifted to Gwen, and Wesley remembered they hadn't met.

"This is the forensic entomologist, Gwyneth Reece. Gwen, this is Detective Walker and Officer Willard."

They shook hands. "Heard a lot about you. Thanks for coming on such short notice."

"Your buddy drives a hard bargain."

"I'll bet he does." Dean shot him a smirk.

"I'm almost done with my examination. As I was just telling Wesley, I'll leave my report with Jessica."

"Have you found anything interesting so far?"

"Actually, yes—"

Wesley interrupted, addressing Dean. "Beyond interesting. Gwen's given us our first lead."

"A lead?"

"Yep. I'll tell you all about it, and you'll tell me what you've got so far. We've got a lot do this afternoon. Let's give Gwen some space to get back to work."

"Okay, let's go talk, then. I could use some coffee."

"Me, too." Wesley paused, hoping for a moment alone with Gwen. When Dean and Willard didn't catch the hint, he turned to her. "Thanks again for coming. You've been extremely helpful. I'll leave your payment up front with Jess."

She stuck out her hand. "Pleasure to meet you, Mr. Cross."

He slid his hand over hers, every sensor in his body reacting to the touch of her skin. They locked eyes, lingering a moment before she released his hand and turned away.

Gwen watched Wesley walk out of the lab with her stomach sinking.

Well, that was it. She'd done her job, and Wesley was gone. What did she expect?

"Hey..." Jessica walked up behind her. "Just wanted to say it's exceptionally impressive what you came up with. I know Wesley badgered you to come, but, really, you've been invaluable to this investigation."

"Thank you, and badgering might be a bit of an over-statement."

Jessica laughed. "Stalking, then."

Gwen smiled. "More accurate."

"Wesley doesn't believe in the word 'no'. If he wants something, he goes and gets it. No matter what it takes. Admirable, yet annoying, if you ask me."

Gwen hesitated, wanting to ask all the questions she had about the mystery that was Wesley Cross but didn't want to push it.

As if reading her thoughts, Jessica continued. "He's a good guy. We've been friends since preschool and I want to make it clear that he had nothing to do with this." She motioned to Leena. "I know the gossip and I know what you might think, but he didn't. I'd bet my life on it."

"I believe that." And she did. She looked at the door, where he'd been standing moments earlier. "What's his deal, anyway?"

"How do you mean?"

"Well, he's probably the most bull-headed person I've ever met, but people seem to trust him. You, with the office here. Gus at the pizza place, and obviously the Detective if he's looping him in on the case. Despite what appears to be a pretty thick dose of cockiness, people seem to like him."

"That's Wesley. He's born and raised here. Knows everyone. He's hardworking, which goes a long way in a small town like this. And loyal. He's just a good guy. A happy-go-lucky kind of guy who doesn't like to see anyone hurt or upset. He'll make an effort to brighten your day if he knows you've had a shit one, you know what I mean? Cocky, sure. But look at the guy. Don't blame him. And he gained a lot of respect, too, when he joined the Marines out of high school."

"Marines?"

Jessica smiled and shook her head. "He didn't tell you. That's just like him. Despite being confident, he doesn't brag, and believe me he has a lot to brag about. He was part of an elite special ops team in the Marines, MARSOC I think they call it. He was top dog. And that gun business of his? Built it from the damn ground up. Blood, sweat, and tears. And after all those years working his ass off, he just signed a multi-million-dollar contract with the government." She snorted. "Our own Wesley Cross, a millionaire, can you believe that? And now... now, look what's happening. Poor Leena, and poor him. Anyway, he's a hard-working son of a bitch and a good guy, and I'll have anyone's hide who says otherwise."

"Why'd he leave the Marines? A woman?"

Jessica laughed. "No. No, no, no. Honestly, I think he wanted to make a different life for himself. What they did, what his team did, was some serious stuff, though he wouldn't tell you that." She laughed again. "No, Wesley hasn't had a serious relationship in his entire life."

Gwen cocked her head. "Come on..."

"Seriously. He... has some issues in the woman department."

"Issues?"

"Yeah. His mom left him and his sister when they were babies. Rumor has it, she ran off with some guy. Never came back." Jessica shook her head. "Wesley loves women, don't get me wrong. He was mister all-star in high school and has been the most popular guy in town since I can remember. Women fall over themselves for him. He's dated half the state, but that's it. *Dated.* Never allows anyone to get close to him. I'm no psychologist but I'm guessin' it's 'cause he doesn't trust them. His mama runnin' off like that. Has to affect someone, ya know?" She took a quick breath. "I've said too much. Anyway, I just wanted to make sure you didn't leave here with any doubt about him, and I wanted to thank you. It was, honestly, a pleasure to meet you."

"Thank you, and you, too."

"I'll leave you alone for real now. We'll chat before you take off."

"Thanks."

She watched Jessica leave the room. Her gaze shifted to the rain-streaked window.

Wesley Cross.

Gwen took a steadying breath as her heart squeezed at the sickening thought that she'd never see him again. But maybe that was for the best. She didn't have time in her life for a relationship, especially for a drop-dead gorgeous alpha male with a body like a Greek God. And besides, he was probably just like all the others. He'd probably cheat on her with the first blonde to bat her eyelashes at him. *Yep,* she thought as she turned away from the window, just like all the others.

... Right?

10

*K*AYLEE JERKED AWAKE at the sound of banging on her door.

What the hell?

She lifted her face from the pillow and with one, blood-shot eye looked at the clock—2:30 p.m.

Holy shit.

She groaned and rolled over, feeling like an eighteen-wheeler had driven over her forehead. She focused on the pitter-patter of rain on her window. She'd only had one, two... was it three martinis at brunch? Her stomach heaved... oh, that's right, and two tequila shots.

She cursed whoever was at her front door, praying that the wrath of God would rain down on them and make them go away.

Dammit, why did she have so many drinks? They were celebrating, that's why. Martinis and hot-pink bridesmaid dresses go hand-in-hand. Besides, it's only once that her best friend, Lydia, gets married. *Once?* Oh hell, who was she kidding? She'd already placed a bet with the other brides-maid, Sam, that the marriage would crash and burn within one year. A bitch move? Probably. But she knew how crazy-possessive Lydia could get, and no man in his right mind would put up with that bullshit twenty-four-seven.

Another bang on the door.

Kaylee pushed off the bed, glanced in the mirror and grimaced at the train wreck staring back at her. After running her fingers through her hair and smoothing her wild eyebrows, she padded to the front door.

She looked out the peephole and frowned. A soaking-wet, middle-aged man in a cowboy hat, wranglers—complete with a shiny buckle—and boots stood on her doorstep glancing at his watch with a scowl on his face. Was she still asleep? Was this a dream? Was she in the middle of some cheesy Western movie? She cocked her head—was he kind of cute? In an old man, rugged cowboy kind of way? His gaze shot up to the peep hole with an icy glare as if he'd read her thoughts.

Okay, no. Definitely not hot.

He raised his fist to knock and before she had to suffer through another *bang*, she opened the door.

"Miss Rhodes?"

"Uh, yeah."

He reached into his pocket and flipped open a badge. "I'm Thomas Grimes, FBI. Mind if I come in for a moment?"

Her eyebrows shot up. *The FBI?!*

Every law she'd broken in the last ten years flashed through her mind as if her life was ending. Was he here about the message she'd spray painted on her ex's barn last week? *Fuck You Asshole* was an expression of free speech, right? Sweat began to bead on her forehead. Or maybe the time she and Lydia skipped out on their fifty-dollar tab at Gino's? Gus had been flirting with her all night, so surely he didn't mind. Or was it about the time they'd stolen Lydia's mom's pot, climbed to the top of the water tower and gotten high? *Oh God*, or maybe...

"I said, mind if I come in for a minute?"

"Uh, yeah, I mean, no... sure." Kaylee stepped back and held open the door as he paused at her foyer. With a stern expression that reminded her of a principal, he quickly skimmed her living room, as if taking a mental inventory of every single thing he saw. She followed his gaze to the empty wine bottle on the coffee table. *Shit.*

"What's the nature of your relationship with the man who visited you yesterday morning?"

Her eyes rounded. "Who? *Lawrence?* He's... uh, he's a friend."

"Just a friend?"

Oh, God. Now she was confused, scared, *and* embarrassed. Her heartbeat kicked started. She stammered, "Um, well, uh, I guess we kinda hook-up from time to time."

The man nodded.

Did he already know that? How?

"How long have you known Mr. Bennett?"

Bennett. She hadn't even known the last name of the guy she was banging. She cringed. Her mom would be so disappointed. "We met at Donny's, a few weeks ago, I guess it was."

"When, exactly?"

She frantically tried to remember the date. "Um, two weeks ago, I think. He'd just moved to town."

"From where?"

"I'm... not sure actually." Her cheeks began to redden with embarrassment.

"Why did he say he came to Berry Springs?"

"He said he loved the area, so he moved here."

"Did he ever mention any friends?"

"No. No names, at all."

"What about plans he might have with people, friends, family?"

Kaylee shook her head. "No, he's never talked about friends or family."

"Not even in the context of telling you how his day was?"

"No..."

Thomas narrowed his eyes and stared at her for a moment, then asked, "Did he talk about his work?"

"What do you mean his work?"

"His job."

"Oh. Just that he works at the Half Moon Hotel. Got a job there a few weeks ago."

He looked around her apartment, again. "Have you been to his place?"

"No, he always comes here."

"How often do you see him?"

How many times had they had sex? "I've seen him four times, that's it."

"Including yesterday morning?"

"Yes."

"How long does he stay each visit?"

"An hour, max." *Or, thirty minutes.*

"What's the nature of your conversations when he visits?"

A bead of sweat rolled down her back. The nature of their conversations revolved around the words, *drop your pants,* and *oh yeah baby,* but there was no way in hell she was going to tell the FBI agent that.

"Um, just small talk, mostly. He really keeps to himself." She looked down, shifted her weight. "Look... we're just kind of each other's booty call, okay? Honestly, I don't know much about him. He isn't really a talker if you know what I mean."

"Did he ever get any calls while he was here?"

"Not that I recall."

The agent stared at her for what seemed like an eternity, then pulled out a card with his number. "If you think of anything else, please call me."

She took the card. "I will."

He turned and paused at the doorway. He ran his finger over the knob and trim. "These locks are a joke, Miss Rhodes. Might want to think about getting some new ones."

The tone of his voice had a chill snaking up her spine.

He closed the door, and Kaylee wrapped her arms around herself and walked to the window. She watched him take one last look at her apartment before folding himself into a dinged-up sedan. He was on his phone the moment he pulled out of her driveway.

She frowned and drew the curtain, baffled by the last five minutes.

Lawrence Bennett?

Kaylee thought of every interaction she'd had with him. Or rather, every time they'd had sex. Had she noticed anything odd about him? Red flags? Had he said anything that surprised her? Why was the FBI asking about the seemingly boring Lawrence Bennett?

She glanced at the clock.

Well, she'd find out tonight, wouldn't she? Lawrence *Bennett* might not be a big talker, but he sure as hell was going to answer some questions tonight.

11

"*L*AST PERSON OUT here got shot at." Wesley walked up to his sister, on her hands and knees in mud, sifting through rocks.

She turned, the rain pouring off her hood. "I knew you'd see my car when you pulled up your driveway." Dark circles shaded her usually bright eyes, accompanied with a puffiness that sent him on alert.

"And besides," she forced a grin and continued. "If you shot at me with the same aim you took at the killer, I'd have nothing to worry about."

He ignored the quip and handed her an umbrella he'd grabbed from the kitchen before taking off through the field in search of his sister. He squatted down next to her. "What's wrong, Bobbi? Why the hell are you out here, in the woods, in the middle of a rainstorm?"

She heaved out a breath and sat back on her heels, the rain splashing around them. "Looking for anything they might've missed. There's got to be something out here."

"You're about a quarter-mile from where the killer parked."

"I know... I've made my way down."

"Bobbi, Willard was out here again this morning, right when the sun came up. They've taken three passes. The damn rain is against us. Leave this to them, okay?"

She looked down.

"Bobbi, what's wrong?"

She shook her head, and he noticed a quiver in her lip. "I don't know, Wes. I couldn't sleep last night. I just..." Her eyes filled with tears. "God, Wes, I couldn't handle it if anything happened to you. I mean, obviously someone has something serious against you. Enough to kill for."

Her tears were like a knife through his heart. "Hey." He lightly grabbed her chin and wiped away the tear running down her cheek. "Don't worry about me, okay? Ever. I can handle it. Shit, B, I've handled a lot worse than this."

"Have you, Wes? Yeah, I know you went through a lot in the Marines, but this is personal. You're all I've got, you know that? Dad... I mean dad is a great guy, but he's not exactly someone I can talk to. And of course, Mom..." Her voice trailed off. "You mean everything to me, brother."

"And you mean everything to me, too, B. You're the only constant in my life. You're my sister. I'm not going anywhere and neither are you, okay? Yeah, Mom left, but so what? We can't change what happened, and bottom-line, I'm not going anywhere. I'll always be here for you. You can take that to the fucking bank."

She sniffed. "And no one's *taking* you from me, either. If anyone wants to hurt you, well, they've got to get through me first." She clenched her jaw and pushed to her feet. "Dammit, look at me, crying like a damn *girl*."

Wesley stood, desperately searching for the right words to calm her down. Seeing his sister upset tore him up. Always had.

"It must be my period. I'm never this weepy."

"*Gross*. B. Gross. I told you..."

"Yeah, I know, that's the one thing I'm not allowed to talk to you about." She inhaled deeply. "Okay, I'm okay. Geez. Get it together, B." She began pacing. "Why don't they have any leads, yet?"

"They do." He took her arm. "Come on. Let's go inside, get some coffee."

She nodded, and as they walked through the woods, he filled her in on Gwen's analysis of the eggs and her theory about the murder weapon.

"What was this girl's name again?"

"Gwyneth Reece."

"I hope you paid Miss Reece well."

He looked down.

Bobbi slapped his arm. "Whoa, whoa, *whoa*, wait a second." She grinned. "You *like* her?"

"What? No. What makes you say that?"

"Oh, I know my brother, and I can see it all over your face."

He felt her giving him the side-eye as they walked in silence for a moment.

"There's just something about her, I guess. She's smart, dedicated to her job, and has an attitude on her like someone else I know." He glanced at Bobbi and winked. "You'd like her. You two would get along."

"Bring her over. Let me meet her, and I'll let you know if she's for you."

"As nice as watching you grill her sounds," he said sarcastically, "she's gone now. Left for the airport hours ago."

"You're going to let that stop you?"

"It's been a hell of an afternoon, B. And I've kinda got a

lot going on right now. Shit, for all I know, she thinks I had something to do with Leena's death."

"Then she's short-sighted and ignorant. But she's not, right? She's not. Give it a chance, Wes." She sighed. "It's time for you to settle down. I *want* you to get married and have babies. I want to be an aunt and teach my nieces and nephews yoga."

"And how to hit a target?" He grinned.

"Well, I guess that's on me after your latest pitiful attempt." She met his grin.

"Hey. The fucker kicked gravel in my face, and the fog was thicker than damn smoke."

"Okay, okay. That's the last time I'll give you crap about it. Anyway, you've got to give someone a chance. If you like this girl... if there was an instant 'thing' you felt, give it a chance. We need more family."

The words hung like heavy weights on his shoulders.

"Hey, right back at you, you know."

"I'm almost a decade younger than you are. My biological clock isn't ticking yet."

He wondered, *was his?* He looked away.

"Now, tell me what Dean and Willard had to say about everything."

Wesley inhaled deeply, thankful to be off the subject of his love life. "Dean assigned Officer Hayes to put together a list of everyone who works at the local sanitation department, the farmer's market vendors, and everyone in the county with a hunting license."

"Hell of a list."

"No shit. Willard knows the local taxidermist personally, so he took that task. Considering I have no power of the state behind me whatsoever, Dean suggested I swing by the animal shelter under the guise of shopping for a new pooch. The shit job, but that was okay; at least I did something."

"Turn up anything?"

"I spoke with everyone there, no red flags for me. Any knife used would be in the clinic and turns out, the vet and vet tech know dad. Ended up talking about fishing for thirty damn minutes, and I don't think either of them had sliced maggot-laden shit and then killed Leena. But I did get the list of people who work at the shelter, and the volunteers."

"How did you get that? Wait... let me guess, the person working the desk was a woman."

"Hey, it's not my fault she was willing to help out. Anyway, Dean said he'd check the pawn shops to see if anyone had purchased a six-inch serrated hunting knife in the last few weeks."

"Good thinking."

"Yep. So, once Dean receives the list from Hayes—he's already got mine—he'll compare it with criminal records, and then compare *that* list with the DMV to see if anyone drives a black SUV. Maybe we'll get a hit."

"It's a start. Finally. Thanks to your girlfriend."

He rolled his eyes, and she laughed, then said, "Okay, that was the last one. Alright, what did Dean and Willard think about doing more DNA testing around Leena's neck?"

"They were skeptical, at best."

"What about her cell phone? Find it yet?"

"No, that or her purse. Dean's hoping to get the data dump by this evening."

"I'll cross my fingers."

"Both hands."

They stepped out of the tree line and onto a dirt road. She stopped. "You think this is the road the guy took to get to the clearing where he parked, right?"

"I don't think, I know. Aside from coming up my driveway and driving through the field, this is the only way to get there."

"And they've checked it, right? Willard has?"

"Willard and Hayes, and now you, apparently."

"Did they find your bullet shells?"

"Two of the four. Guessin' the rain washed the others. We'll find 'em."

She started to kneel down to search again, but he grabbed her arm. "No, Bobbi, come on. Let them handle it. You're soaked. Let's get you inside."

"Okay, okay, okay."

And as he pulled her along with him, he didn't notice the blood-stained rock beside her boot.

Two hours and three inches of rain later, Wesley eyed his rearview mirror, squinting to see through the rain-streaked back windshield of his truck. The dreary light of day was fading, making seeing through the monsoon even more difficult. A blue sedan drove directly behind him, and behind that, a dark-colored SUV.

Was it black?

Was he being followed?

He flicked on his turn signal and turned into a residential neighborhood. He slowed down, his eyes locked on the rearview mirror. The SUV slowly passed the road, then disappeared. He did a U-turn, and shot back onto the road, hoping to catch the license plate, but the vehicle was gone.

Humph.

He circled the square, eyeing each vehicle, then decided to give up. He didn't even know if the damn thing was black, and besides, he had somewhere else he needed to get to. He hit a red light and pulled out his cell phone.

Over the last four hours, Wesley had checked his phone more times than he'd like to admit, hoping Gwen would call with news, or maybe call to tell him she was wearing nothing but a cherry-red thong and thinking of him. She hadn't. And as he pulled into the small parking lot in front of D.D.'s Jewelry Store, he checked it one more time.

He peered through the rain, shocked to see the neon *Open* sign flashing in the window. Not only because the store had been closed all day—he knew this because he'd driven by five times already—but because it was pushing seven o'clock in the evening.

Wesley reached into his pocket and grasped the bracelet. He still hadn't told Dean that he'd taken it from Leena's wrist, or about the mysterious pendant he'd discovered on it. Not until he did a little investigative work on his own, at least. And this was step one.

A bell jingled above his head as he pushed through the front door.

"Just a minute!" This from somewhere in the back.

Wesley smiled at the familiar voice. D.D. Wreckers, or Mrs. D.D. as she was known around town, had owned and operated D.D.'s Jewelry Store for as long as he could remember. Somewhere in her mid-seventies, D.D. was a quick-witted, no-bullshit kind of woman who began every morning with a two-mile walk, and ended every evening with a gin and ginger ale. She'd recently hired Wesley to make a custom gun for her husband, and they'd developed a friendship. He was relieved to see her working and not her husband, who only filled in for her occasionally and surely wouldn't be able to answer the questions he had.

The five-foot-one-inch woman hobbled out of the back room. Her eyes lit up the moment she saw him.

"Well, my dear Wesley Cross!"

"Hey there, Mrs. D.D." He frowned at the walking cast on her foot. "What happened?"

"Sprained my damn ankle tripping over one of Tom's damn walking sticks. Goddamned walking sticks. Collects them, he does."

"I'm sure you gave him hell about it."

The old woman snorted. "Hell would've been easier on him. Anyway, he's out of town today, and I had to get my own self to the doctor."

"Mrs. D.D., you can always call me for things like that."

"I know that, dear."

"Where's he at?"

"Some gun show downstate, been gone since Friday morning. Three nights now. Three nights of bliss." She winked and braced herself on the glass counter that separated them. Inside lay dozens of gold rings and chains illuminated under yellow light.

"He should be back this evening, and then it's back to fetching his beer and listening to the damn news on blast. I swear I've considered getting earplugs." She braced the edge, leaning her weight against it. "How you holdin' up, kid?"

So the gossips had already gotten to her. "Okay. It'll pass."

"Yes, sir, it most certainly will. I promise you that. In the meantime, I've got your back, son. Anyone talkin' shit, I've been settin' them straight."

Anyone accusing him of murder, she meant.

"You don't need to do that."

"I sure do. You're a good kid, Wesley. Always thought so.

They'll catch the son of a bitch, and this will all be behind you. Although, if I know anything about you, you've got your own investigation going on behind the scenes. If you need anything, you let me know. Okay?"

He smiled. "Thanks."

"Anyway..." She cocked her head. "What brings you in today?"

He pulled the bracelet from his pocket, secured in a plastic baggie. "There's a pendant on this. I'm hoping you recognize it? Maybe sold it from your store?"

She took it from his hands and something flickered in her eyes as she examined it.

"And the gemstone, is that emerald?" He asked.

Wesley watched her closely as she pulled down the glasses from the top of her head and flipped the magnifier down. She turned the bracelet over in her fingers several times. Her hand froze. She paused and looked up at him.

"There's blood on the hemp, son."

His eyes leveled on hers. "Yes, ma'am."

She stared at him for a moment, then gave a quick nod, a nonverbal acceptance to keep her mouth shut, and began examining it again. "The green gem... no, it couldn't be..."

"What? Couldn't be what?"

"Just a minute..." D.D.'s voice trailed off as she disappeared into the office. A minute later, she returned with a thick, black binder. She plopped it on the glass counter, a puff of dust wafting up from the sides. After what felt like fifty pages of searching, her finger landed on a picture of a green stone.

"Yep. Thought so. Chrome Diopside."

"Chrome what?"

"Diopside." She turned the binder to face him. "See here?"

His eyes skimmed the description on the page.

"Very rare gemstone. It's a pretty pendant." She picked up the bracelet again. "Whoever attached it did a poor job. Thing's about to fall off."

"Do you sell it here?"

"No, never have. Never carried anything with Diopside, either. Like I said, it's pretty rare."

"Has anyone come in asking for it?"

"No. Not that I can recall."

"Is it sold anywhere local?"

She chewed on her lower lip. "No, don't think so."

Humph.

They both stared in silence at the bracelet.

"Wait... wait, yes, I think I remember someone selling a necklace with Chrome Diopside a while ago. Yes..." she slowly nodded, validating her epiphany. "Yes, that little jewelry shop in the Half Moon Hotel." She scowled. "I wish they'd do something with that place. Just sitting on that cliff out in the middle of nowhere. Creepy if you ask me. Anyway, yes, a woman by the name of Sofia runs the shop." D.D. narrowed her eyes and set down the bracelet. "Don't go buyin' anything from her, though. Anything she has, I can order for half the cost, okay?"

Sofia. He nodded. "Yes, ma'am." He grabbed the bracelet from the counter. "Thank you, D.D."

"Of course. You let me know if you need anything, okay? And if you go there, watch out for the ghosts. That place is haunted, you know."

He smiled. "Will do. Thanks, again."

Wesley jumped into his truck and pulled out his phone.

"Hello, Jessica Heathrow."

"Jess, it's Wesley."

"Hey. I don't have any more info for you yet—"

"I know, I know. This is... I have a favor to ask of you."

Pause. "What kind of favor?"

"Like, we've known each other since birth kind of favor." He pulled onto the road.

"So a big favor."

"Yeah. I've got a bracelet. I need you to scan it for fingerprints."

"Wesley." Her voice stone-cold now. "Where did you get this bracelet?"

"Telling you might get you in trouble. Ignorance will keep your hands clean, trust me."

"Wesley..." she groaned. "I don't like the sound of this."

"There's a pendant on it that I think was attached by someone other than the owner of the bracelet. Focus on that. But you'll find my prints all over it, too, unfortunately."

A minute ticked by.

"Jess? I really need this. If you don't find anything, we'll just pretend this never happened. If you do, you will have solved a murder."

"Wesley, if you took it from a crime scene, regardless of what I find, it won't be admissible—"

"I *know*. I fucked up, alright?" He heaved out a breath. "Please, Jess."

A deep sigh, then, "Okay, Wesley. I'll do what I can."

"Thank you, Jess... *thank you*."

"Alright, swing it by, and I'll get right on it."

"Be there in five, but hey..."

"Oh, God, what?"

"There's blood on it, just FYI."

"Leena's," she whispered.

"Ignorance is bliss, Jess. See you in five."

12

*L*IGHTNING PIERCED THE sky, followed by a bellow of thunder that he swore shook his truck as Wesley ascended the tallest mountain in Berry Springs. Dead leaves tumbled across the windshield.

Hell of a storm, indeed.

There was no dusk to marvel at on the horizon, no bright colors of yellow, orange and pink to celebrate the end of the day. Only a muted, eerie glow across the mountains.

He glanced at the clock—7:36 p.m.

Wesley hadn't passed a single car since he'd left the city limits. Everyone was home, hunkered down, staying out of the weather, which was getting worse by the minute. He clicked on the local radio station.

"... *strong line of storms moving at thirty miles an hour ahead of the front. Two tornadoes have already been reported. Heavy lightning, high winds, hail, and flash flooding is expected with these storms. I repeat, if you're not home, please get there or take shelter. Stay away from windows and prepare a safe place. We've already received four inches of rain, so please take caution over bridges as flooding has already been reported. The storms should subside after midnight, but we're not done, folks. We're under a dense fog advisory until nine tomorrow morning. Bottom line, get home and keep NAR News close by. We'll be here to keep you updated all night."*

He turned on his high beams, contemplating. Well, he was almost there. No turning back now.

The Half Moon Hotel was located on the peak of Summit Mountain, surrounded by miles and miles of woods. The hotel was legendary in Berry Springs and had been featured in several national documentaries. Built in the mid-eighteen hundreds, the four-story hotel was originally built as a hospital, specializing in mental health with an in-house assisted living facility. Thirty years later, a wealthy oil heir purchased it and turned it into one of the most luxurious resorts in the region, attracting adventure seekers from all across the county. But no matter how much good press it received, the hotel couldn't shake the rampant rumor that its halls were haunted by the patients who were treated badly, even murdered during their treatment years earlier. Over the decades, the hotel had been renovated several times, but still maintained the "old-world" feel with antique furniture and fixtures throughout. *Creepy*, as D.D. had said, and he completely agreed.

Wesley slammed the brakes as he came to the river, its raging waters less than a foot from the bottom of the rickety, one-lane bridge that crossed it. Flash flooding was right.

Holy shit.

He hesitated on crossing, but knew there was no way in hell he was going to be able to sleep until he spoke with Sofia and hopefully—*hopefully*—get the name of whoever had recently purchased the pendant. Wouldn't be the first time he'd lost a truck to the river.

Wesley slowly accelerated over the bridge. The wood creaked and groaned beneath his truck, and he made a mental note to tell Dean to get someone to fix the damned thing. It was a miracle it hadn't already collapsed—rain or not.

After making it to the other side, Wesley navigated his way through the windy mountain road until he came to a wooden sign that read *Welcome to the Half Moon Hotel*. Antique light posts lit the way as he crested the mountain and the hotel came into view, its lights twinkling through the haze of rain. A lightning bolt flashed diagonally across the sky, barely missing the peaks of the fourth floor. Of all the nights to be visiting a place on the top of a mountain.

The front of the hotel had a covered circle drive underneath columns that stretched up to the fourth-floor balcony bar, where stone gargoyles peered angrily at the property below. Even in the light of day, the hotel had a creep factor, but with the dark clouds, rain, lightning, and thunder, it rivaled any haunted house in his childhood nightmares.

Wesley had only been inside a handful of times, once as a teenager to take the haunted tour on Halloween night, once to attend a wedding, and a few times he'd hit the fourth-floor bar with a few buddies. Hell of a view, especially after a few drinks.

He searched for a place to park, noting several blocked-off areas with construction equipment. They were renovating again, apparently. He settled for a spot at the end of a row, hugging the woods. He shoved the truck into park and checked the time—7:44 p.m. He'd better hustle if he had any chance of visiting the jewelry store. After grabbing his cell phone and wallet, Wesley sprinted across the parking lot and up the blood-red carpeted steps that led to the front doors. He was greeted by a dark-haired kid who he guessed was just a few years out of high school.

"Sir."

Wesley nodded, his gaze skimming the lobby. He froze as their eyes met across the room. *No freaking way.* He ground his teeth.

Shit, shit, shit.

"Sir? Can I help you with something?" The bellman asked.

He tore his eyes away from the platinum blonde in a skin-tight shirt and cowboy boots bee-lining it to him. "Uh, yeah, sorry. There's a jewelry store in here, right?"

"Yes, sir, basement level, next to the spa." The young man motioned to the staircase behind him.

"Thanks." He sidestepped the bellman, hoping to disappear before—

"Wesley *freakin'* Cross."

Dammit. He stopped, turned, and was toe-to-toe with Kaylee Rhodes. As if on cue, thunder boomed outside.

"Hey, Kaylee." He forced a smile as he looked down at one of Leena Ross's former best friends, and one of his former girlfriends.

Wesley and Kaylee had dated for about two months, over a decade ago, when he was less committed to being one-hundred percent non-committal. She was a southern spit-fire with a temper that had become legendary in Berry Springs. When they'd cooled, she couldn't let go, calling him every name in the book and spent most of the following month driving by his house at all hours of the evening. But it wasn't until Kaylee had caught him flirting with her friend, Lydia Hess, that she'd broken into his house and trashed the place. By all counts, she was a crazy woman. A crazy woman whom he avoided at all costs. A crazy woman who now stood two inches from him, staring daggers into his eyes.

"Is there any news? Tell me. What do you know?"

He shook his head. "I can't get into that."

"You can't get into that? She was one of my best friends, Wesley!"

"I'm sorry, Kaylee. Really, I am."

She snorted. "Yeah, I bet you are. What're you doin' here, anyway? Shouldn't you be at the *station* or something?"

In jail, she meant. He narrowed his eyes, his patience waning. "Just taking the scenic route home."

"Yeah, right." She popped her gum, eyeing him.

He took a step closer to the staircase and considered throwing himself down it.

"Well, *we're* here for Lydia's bridesmaid party," she continued. "Booked the spa all day tomorrow... we were gonna cancel, ya know, considering, but we put down a deposit and all."

He nodded and pressed his lips together. The fewer words he spoke to this woman, the better.

She glowered at him. "Hey, just because Leena and I had a falling out years ago doesn't mean I don't care about her death, *Wesley.*"

"None of my business. Now, if you'll excuse—"

She shoved her hands on her hips. "Heard they formally interviewed you."

"Tends to happen when a body is found in someone's house."

"A *body*. You're a son of a bitch, you know that? Always were. I should've never dated you. You're such an *asshole.*"

Pick your battles, Wesley reminded himself, and a battle with a drunk cowgirl was not one he was willing to have at that moment. So he bit his tongue and turned away. "See ya, Kaylee."

"Yeah, you will." She muttered as her bedazzled cowboy boots stomped away.

He'd had enough damn insinuations for one day. He needed his deck and a stiff drink. And as soon as he spoke with Sofia at the jewelry store, he was going to do just that.

Wesley took the curve in the staircase, the wooden planks creaking underneath him and the muffled chatter above him fading away. The smell of wet earth and eucalyptus filled his nose as he stepped onto the hardwood floors that lined the dimly lit basement level. Other than the distant hum of something in the distance, an air-conditioner maybe, the floor was dead silent. He paused at the bottom of the staircase and looked from left to right. In a velvet armchair facing the windows, an elderly man in a golf cap and polyester checkered suit read the newspaper.

Watching the storm, he thought.

He shifted his gaze to a sign hanging on the wall with arrows pointing in the direction of *Rooms 101-121,The Spa, Ghost Tours*, and, to the right, *Half Moon Jewelry*. At the end of the hall hung a sign that said *Staff Only*. He turned right and followed the worn China rugs that ran down the hall, stopping in front of a small shop with a rainbow of colors dancing on the walls from the crystals that hung from the ceiling.

Wesley pushed through the glass door that read *Half Moon Jewelry*. The room was ripe with freshly burned incense, and the low melody of flutes and chimes broke the silence. The walls were lined with glass shelves filled with decorative rocks and crystals, fairy statues, and burners. Wind chimes hung from the ceiling next to sparkling suncatchers.

He appeared to be the only one in the shop.

He walked to the front counter that held dozens of earrings, necklaces and bracelets; bent over, and searched for the bright green gemstone.

"May I help you?"

Wesley straightened and turned, startled at the voice behind him that came out of nowhere. The woman—he guessed in her mid-sixties—wore a long tie-dyed dress with deep colors of navy and red, and stacks of jewels on her wrists and neck. Her long gray hair ran in dreadlocks down her back. Her skin was a milky pale, highlighting her deep red lips.

"I'm looking for Sofia."

"Yeah? What do you want with her?"

"I hear she works here?"

"She does."

"Is she in today?"

"Why?"

Christ. Why was everything so damn difficult today?

"Ma'am, I just have a question for her about some jewelry. Is she in? I can come back later."

"You're looking at her." Keeping her gaze locked on him, the woman—Sofia, apparently—crossed the room and stepped behind the counter. "How can I help you?"

He zeroed in on the necklace at the nape of her neck, decorated with little, green stones.

"Do you sell cross pendants?"

"A few." She motioned to counter.

"With Chrome Diopside gemstones?"

Her eyes sparked, and a tingle of adrenaline slid up his spine. He was onto something, he could feel it in his bones. Sofia looked past him, then down at the jewelry counter, then another flicker of a glance behind him.

"No," she said, finally. "I don't think so."

"Who orders the jewelry for the store?"

"I do."

"And you don't remember if you've ever ordered a pendant with a gem as rare as Diopside?"

"I order a lot of things Mr..."

"Cross." He leaned forward. "That's a beautiful necklace you've got on. The one with the green gemstones."

Her brows arched as her hand slowly slid up to her neck. A moment ticked by as they stared at each other.

With narrowed eyes, she finally said, "I might have sold Diopside pendants in the past. You'll have to forgive me, I don't remember everything that comes through my store."

"Have you sold any lately?"

Her gaze slid over his shoulder, again. She was either looking for someone, or scared of something. Either way, Wesley's interest was piqued.

"Not that I recall, no."

"Maybe your sales receipts will recall. Surely you keep records of every sale, correct?"

"Are you a cop, Mr. Cross?"

"Yes," he lied, and to keep her from asking for a badge, he quickly said, "I can wait here while you check." He nodded toward the office behind her, which had a small desk, computer, and two file cabinets.

She stared at him another moment, then turned and disappeared into the office. He watched her closely, making sure she knew he was watching her. A minute later, she came out with a piece of paper and laid it on the counter.

"I sold a pendant necklace..."

He looked at the date on the paper. "Three days ago."

"Yes. It had multiple pendants. A few were crosses with

Chrome Diopside. It had been in my shop awhile... which is why it didn't ring a bell. Sorry."

He desperately skimmed the receipt looking for a name. "To who?"

"Don't have that on record."

No name. The necklace was paid for with a credit card but, unfortunately, the first twelve of the sixteen numbers were X's. He memorized the last four.

"Was it a man or a woman?"

She shrugged and he felt his patience dissolving.

"Do you have another employee that possibly sold it?"

"No. Just me here."

"You don't remember if you sold the necklace to a man or a woman? That's a nice chunk of change. You really don't remember?"

"I'm sorry."

Wesley glanced around the room—not a single security camera.

"Where do you get your jewelry? Do you remember where you got the necklace, specifically?"

"My jewelry comes from all over. Sometimes I order it, sometimes I buy in bulk when I travel, and sometimes I make it myself. I might've got the necklace..." She reached up and touched her neck, again. "And this one when I visited Moscow last year. Come to think of it, I'm sure that's where I got the necklace. Chrome Diopside is only found in Russia."

He froze. "Did you say Russia?"

She nodded.

"Are you sure?"

"Yes, I'm fairly certain." The phone rang. "I've got to get that, and I'm sorry, I don't have any more information for you, Officer."

"Thanks, Sofia. I have a feeling I'll see you again."

Wesley's mind raced as he stepped into the hall.

Russia.

He pulled his cell phone from his pocket and checked the calendar. His stomach dropped as he looked at the date.

No fucking way.

His head was spinning as he brought up his contacts, and dialed an old friend.

"Steele Security."

"Steele Security? What the hell is that?"

A pause, then, "Wesley *fucking* Cross, is that you?"

Wesley chuckled. "Yep. How are ya, Gage?"

"Well, holy shit, man. I haven't talked to you in years... Which means you need something."

Nothing got past Gage. "Can't I call just to say hi? What the hell is Steele Security, anyway? You leave the Marines?"

"Yep, three years ago. Started a personal security firm. Hell of a lot better than MARSOC, man."

"Don't doubt that. Personal security, huh? So, what? You spend your days following supermodels around?"

"Sometimes." He was dead serious. "We contract with the government mostly. Head up security details for politicians, eyewitnesses, you know the drill."

Yeah, he knew the drill.

Steele continued, "I'm looking for another man... you interested?"

"Thanks, but I've got my own thing goin'. Guns."

"No shit? You finally did it? Started your own company?"

"Yep."

"Good for you. Good on ya." He paused. "So, you're not looking for a job. Doesn't sound like you've got money problems, or are strung out on drugs. I have no doubt you've got plenty of female problems but God knows I ain't helping you with those crazy bitches. So, what do you need, man?"

"Mikhail Lutrova. You remember that whole deal, right?"

"Of course I remember that whole deal. The sick Russian psychopath caught by the one and only Wesley Cross. Yeah, dude, I remember."

"I didn't catch him. Just supplied the evidence that led the FBI to him. Luck was what it was."

"How many life sentences did he end up getting?"

"Two. One for each girl he murdered. Anyway, you remember that social worker you used to date?"

"Ah, hell... uh, Shelly, I think."

"That's the one. I was hoping you could get Lutrova's file from her."

"Why you want his file?"

"Just some light evening reading, you know."

Gage laughed. "Alright, keep your secrets. I'll see what I can do, but I think she left a while ago. Some dude name Kenneth took her place." He laughed, "In that case, maybe I'll use one of my supermodels to get it out of him."

"You always were resourceful."

"With women? Not like you, man."

"Call me if you get that file."

"Will do."

Click.

Wesley tapped the phone on his chin, a ball forming in his gut. He stared into the raging storm outside recalling the not-too-distant memories from five years earlier.

Berry Springs was in a state of panic after two women had mysteriously gone missing, just days apart. Both women had gone for a jog on the mountain trails and were never seen or heard from again. Both women in their mid-twenties, with dark brown hair and lean, slender bodies.

Bobbi had just opened her indoor/outdoor shooting range and, to her delight, was busier than expected. Wesley had offered to help out until things died down a bit. He'd worked the morning rush, then went back to his shop to make a dent in his own work. Later that evening, he'd decided to swing by for a quick check-in on his way into town to meet some friends at Gino's.

And that last-minute decision just might have saved his sister's life.

It was just past six-thirty, thirty minutes to closing time when he walked through the front doors. He spotted Bobbi behind a glass counter filled with hunting knives, and a tall, bulky man with short, blonde hair, almost as white as snow. The man, Wesley pinned as pushing thirty, was standing to the side, leaning his elbows against the glass, with one leg behind the counter as if he was inching his way around. Wesley's back straightened like a rod, an instinct that something wasn't right. And that instinct was confirmed when Bobbi saw him and relief flashed in her eyes. He quickly made his way across the shop, weaving in-between the racks filled with sporting goods, hunting gear, and bows and arrows.

The man turned, his bloodshot, beady eyes locking on him as he walked up. Wesley remembered the chill that ran up his spine as he looked into those wild, ice-blue eyes. There was something sinister—feral—behind them. He didn't recognize the man but had a feeling he was about to get to know him on a very personal level.

With his eyes locked on the icy man, Wesley addressed Bobbi. "Everything okay here, sis?"

"Yes, Mr. Lutrova—Mikhail—was just leaving."

As she spoke, Wesley had noticed fresh scratches down the man's arms, red scabbed streaks, just below the Russian flag he had tattooed on his forearm.

"Mr. Lutrova, time to pack up," he said.

They stared at each other, and Wesley's fingers itched to grabbed the SIG on his belt. Without a word, the man glanced at Bobbi, lingered a moment, then grabbed his carrying case and slowly walked out of the shop.

He remembered the look on Bobbi's face as the door clicked closed. His usually confident, badass sister had been scared. Seriously scared.

"Who was that?" He asked.

She shrugged, shook her head. "Been in here shooting for two and a half hours. *Two and a half hours.* Didn't talk to anyone, nothing. Just *boom, boom, boom.* Guy must've had a whole bag of ammo. I didn't think much of it until I kept catching him looking at me. Staring at me, like. When the place cleared out and he was still here... I almost called you. He just totally creeped me out, ya know?"

"What was he doing when I walked up?"

"Wanted to see a hunting knife I had behind the counter."

"Looked like he was trying to get behind the counter."

"Exactly. I noticed it, too. My sixth-sense was screaming at me, so I told him I needed to close up early and asked him to leave. He didn't move. And, literally, that's exactly when you walked in."

"Did you see the scratches all over his arms?"

She nodded. "A few down his neck, too."

Wesley's attention shifted to the low hum of the television in the background.

"...again, if anyone has any information on the missing women, please contact local authorities immediately."

"Be right back." He turned, jogged across the shop and burst through the door just as two red tail lights faded into the distance.

He watched the lights until they disappeared, his mind reeling. He walked back into the shop. "What lane was he in?" He yelled across the room.

"Uh, six," Bobbi shouted back.

Wesley entered the shooting range. The floor had been swept, the shells dumped into cans next to each lane. He kneeled down by the can in lane six and plucked the top shells from the pile. He took them home, and using a new ballistics technology that captures a 3D image of a bullet casing and records the unique marks from the firing pin, Wesley scanned each shell he'd taken from the lane and got a hit. A shell with the same markings had been confiscated from a robbery at a local pharmacy a week earlier. Hours later, police raided the home of Mikhail Lutrova.

And that's how the missing women were found, their tortured corpses chained to the wall in an underground cellar, deep in the woods.

Lutrova was arrested, charged, and transported to the state prison where he'd live out the remainder of his life. He was only thirty-three years old.

Later, Wesley had learned that Mikhail was born in Russia and moved to the US with his mother when he was just three years old. They had settled in a small town in Missouri, where his mother married an abusive drug addict. His mom eventually took off, and after child services took him away from his abusive step-father, Mikhail moved in with his grandmother, an hour outside of Berry Springs. Rumor was, Mikhail was a quiet kid who only spoke when spoken to, kept to himself, and had never gotten into any trouble... until he crossed paths with Wesley Cross.

That was five years ago.

Wesley tore his gaze away from the window and pictured the pendant with the little green gemstone, only found in Russia.

Russia.

Was it possible Mikhail Lutrova had something to do with Leena's death?

Wesley shook his head. Or maybe *he* was just going crazy. Reaching. Grasping onto anything to find the son of a bitch that killed her.

He hesitated, then turned on his cell phone—*better safe than sorry*.

"Hey, Wes."

"Hey, Bobbi. Hey, uh…"

"Oh, God, what?"

He ran his fingers through his hair. "Listen. I want you to be vigilant until the guy who killed Leena is caught, okay? Keep your alarm on at all times. Carry your gun; keep it handy, not buried at the bottom of that backpack you call a purse. Be aware and alert when you're walking to and from your car. Just be smart, okay? Anything seems off, walk away."

"What's going on?" Her voice was sharp.

"I just don't want you involved in this whole thing. There's a killer running around Berry Springs and I'm just telling you to be smart."

"Do you think I'm in danger?"

"Technically, every woman in town is until this guy's caught."

"Where are you?"

"The Half Moon Hotel."

"What the hell are you doing there? In this damn storm?"

"Don't worry about it."

"Wes, are *you* in trouble?"

"No, B. Never."

A long pause. "Okay, I will, I promise."

"Good. Thanks. I'll swing by on my way home to check in. Turn on your alarm now. See you soon."

13

*W*ESLEY STEPPED ONTO the lobby level and froze in his tracks.

He knew that long, silky brown hair. He knew that God-awful all-weather hiking jacket and he definitely knew that round, perky little ass.

Not twenty feet ahead of him, Gwyneth Reece stood at the check-in counter with a purse slung over her shoulder and a suitcase at her side, and based on the cocked angle of her hip, she'd brought her attitude as well.

A spark of excitement warmed him as he crossed the room.

"Thought you were headed home."

She turned, startled, a pink flush on her cheeks and streaks of rain in her hair. A small smile crossed her beautiful face—but only for a second, as if she was embarrassed she'd been caught happy to see him.

She nodded toward the storm outside. "I tried to go home. Drove to the airport and sat there for three hours trying to get on the next flight out. Apparently, airplanes don't fly in lightning, and I'm not driving eight hours in this deluge. Especially in the dark."

He soaked in every inch of her face as she spoke. What were the freaking odds?

She continued, "This was the only hotel within forty-five miles with a vacancy."

"That'll be two-hundred and twenty-seven dollars, ma'am," the receptionist said.

"Geez."

As she reached into her purse, Wesley tossed his credit card on the counter.

"No, Wesley—"

"Wes."

Gwen shook her head, clearly annoyed. "No, Wes. You can't..."

With a flirty smile, the receptionist handed him back his card.

He smiled. "Thank you."

Gwen sighed. "Seriously, you didn't have to do that."

He slid his wallet back into his pocket. "Yes, I did. You're here because of me. It's my pleasure to pay for you to stay in this luxurious castle for a night." He winked.

She snorted, then cocked her head. "What are you doing here, anyway?"

"Just following up on some things."

"Room four-twenty-eight, ma'am, top floor." The receptionist packed an envelope. "Your key's inside, as well as restaurant, spa, entertainment, and in-room dining information." As she handed the envelope to Gwen, the dark-haired, blue-eyed receptionist batted her long, faux eyelashes at Wesley. He raised his eyebrows.

She finally looked back at Gwen. "Will you be going to the ball tonight?"

"Ball?"

"Yes. Four times a year, the Half Moon Hotel has a ball to celebrate the turn of the season. Dresses, tuxedos, music, dancing. The works. It's a lot of fun." She glanced at the clock. "Starts at eight, so just a few minutes. Usually lasts 'til midnight or so, but that's when it's packed... it might cut off earlier tonight."

"No, I don't think I'll be attending."

Gwen said it without hesitation, which should have surprised him, but didn't. While most women loved to dress up and go dancing, Gwen didn't seem the type. She was different. Refreshingly so. While most girls screamed at the mere sight of a bug, Gwen had made an entire career out of them.

The receptionist shrugged. "You really should consider it. You might have the ball to yourself, with how few people are here right now."

"I noticed. Why is that?" Wesley asked.

"We're about to do renovations. We have over half the rooms blocked off to begin moving furniture out. Combine that with the weather, and I think there's less than ten people here tonight."

"Ten people?"

"'Round there. Might get more as the night goes on. Anyway, the ball is a lot of fun... kind of brings you back to the old times before dancing and chivalrous men were replaced by video games and dating apps. Anyway, there's a dress shop downstairs if you change your mind. My name's Melanie Jones," another flirty glance at him and this time Gwen's eyebrows tipped up. "Please let me know if you need anything. I hope you enjoy your stay."

"Thank you, Melanie." Gwen's voice was clipped, and Wesley couldn't help but wonder if it was because of the fact he'd paid for her room or because of the receptionist's notice of him.

As they turned away, Wesley grabbed her bag.

"Do you have that effect on all women?"

That answered his question. Gwen didn't like another woman noticing him. And he liked that.

"Depends," he responded. "Do I have that effect on you, Miss Reece?"

"Takes a little more than a nice smile and jacked-up body for me, Mr. Cross." She flipped through the brochure.

"Then, I guess not. Hang right here for a minute, okay?"

Busy skimming the room-service menu in a thinly veiled effort to make sure he knew that she didn't notice his "nice smile," she gave him a slight nod.

He turned toward the receptionist. "Hey, Melanie?"

"Yes?"

He set his elbows on the counter and leaned forward, locking eyes with the receptionist. "Would you mind checking on something for me real quick?"

"Of course, Mr. Cross."

"I found a receipt for a pricey piece of jewelry on the floor downstairs. Dropped by accident, I assume. I have the last four digits of the credit card; can you tell me a name, or if the person is staying here?"

"Oh, uh... I don't think..."

"I bet it's just a quick search for you. If it's too much trouble, though..."

"Oh, no, not at all. Uh, sure, I can do that. What are they?"

He rattled off the numbers. She clicked a few keys, then frowned. "*Hmm*, no one's reserved a room with a credit card ending in those four digits."

Dammit. "Okay, thank you, Melanie."

He winked, she giggled, and he turned back toward Gwen. "I can carry your bag to your room for you."

Gwen glanced up from the map of the grounds. Interesting reading, apparently.

"No, I've got to move my rental car. I parked under the balcony so I wouldn't get wet." She looked down at her boots, soaked at the toe. "Worked out real well as you can see."

"I'm parked below. I'll drive you back up after you park."

"Okay." Her gaze flickered toward the receptionist. "Thanks."

Wesley handed her bag to the bellman. "What's your name?"

The freckled, redheaded kid squared his shoulders. "James, sir."

"James, I'm—"

"Wesley Cross. I know who you are." The kid glanced out the window as a limo pulled up.

Wesley cocked his head. "Yeah? How so?"

"Seen you around. My dad's mentioned you before. Think he bought one of your guns."

Wesley stared at James for a moment, trying to decide if the kid liked him, or didn't. Or maybe he just didn't approve that Wesley made guns for a living, like a lot of kids in the twenty-something generation.

"What's your dad's name?"

"Trace." The bellman's attention pulled to a man and woman walking up the steps with an armful of bags. "I gotta get the door."

"Would you mind watching Miss Reece's bag for a moment while we park her car?"

"Will do. Just set it over there."

"Thanks." Wesley stepped past a particularly busty

woman griping to her husband about the weather, a cloud of perfume following a second later. He opened the door for Gwen and stepped outside. It was as dark as midnight and the buzz of the rain was so loud that it drowned out everything else. The weather was getting worse, no doubt about that.

"That was kind of odd." Gwen looked at him.

Wesley glanced over his shoulder at James, who was on his phone watching them through the window. "Yeah it was, wasn't it?"

"You know his dad?"

"Some random dude named Trace? Nope."

"Should've asked a last name."

"Can't be too hard to figure out."

"That's right, just ask your girlfriend behind the reception desk."

"Jealous?" He winked.

She snorted and avoided the question. "Here's my car."

He opened the door for her, then slid into the passenger seat as she settled behind the wheel.

"My truck's just down this hill."

Hail pinged the windshield as she drove out from under the covered circle drive.

"Holy smokes." She looked at him. "I hope you got renter's insurance."

"I like living on the edge."

Lightning popped in the sky.

"Geez, do I need to worry about a tornado or something?"

"In this place? No way. The basement is solid rock."

"I mean, is there a warning or anything?"

"Doubt it." Although he hadn't checked the weather in hours.

She rolled to a stop behind his truck. "Be careful."

Wesley laughed and jumped out. Hail hammered the top of his head, a few pellets sliding past his collar as he jogged around to his truck.

He stopped dead in his tracks.

He wasn't going anywhere.

Because all four of his tires had been slashed.

14

*G*WEN FROWNED AS she peered through the blurry windshield. Why had Wesley stopped all of the sudden? What was he staring at? She flicked on the high beams. The wipers made a pathetic swipe against the windshield, clearing just enough to make out the steely look in his eyes.

Something was wrong.

She followed his gaze and peered over the steering wheel. Her mouth dropped. Wesley Cross's expensive, jacked-up truck was sitting on four flat tires.

What the hell?

Gwen watched him slowly walk around the truck as the rain pounded his shoulders. His jaw was set, his fists clenched at his side. He squatted down at each tire, then got into the cab, rummaged around for a minute and then slid something in the back of his pants before grabbing a flannel shirt from the passenger seat.

A *gun?*

Wesley climbed out, took one more circle around the truck, then got into the SUV.

"What happened?"

"Someone slashed my tires."

"What? No way. Are you sure it's not just flats?"

"It's a thin slice on the *side* of each tire." He looked at her. "And besides, four flats at the same time?"

She looked away. Okay, that was stupid. "Who would do that?"

Wesley glanced over his shoulder at the hotel, all lit up at the top of the hill. "Not sure, but I intend to find out."

Gwen looked at his waistband where he'd attempted to hide the fact that he'd grabbed a gun.

"I saw you take a gun from the glovebox."

He ignored her comment as he stared at his truck, deep in thought.

"Why a gun?"

His gaze cut to her. "Better safe than sorry. Okay, let's—"

"You think this is connected to Leena's murder."

He let the comment hang in the air and she got the feeling he wasn't telling her something.

"Either way, whoever slashed my tires is in that hotel." He said.

"Meaning... whoever killed Leena is possibly in the hotel?"

Avoiding her question, he pulled out his cell phone. Yeah, the man definitely wasn't telling her something.

She stared at him as he dialed, trying to process everything that was happening, but more so, trying to understand the man sitting next to her. Handsome, charismatic, happy-go-lucky, bull-headed. But from the moment she'd told him her theory about the murder weapon, she saw glimpses of the military man Jessica had told her about—a relentless, take-no-prisoners man on a mission that not even a thousand bullets could stop. And now, with the gun securely on his hip, it was as if he'd dealt with countless situations like this before. As if he was almost comfortable in this kind of scenario.

The call connected and she listened intently to his side of the conversation.

"Dean, it's Wesley... not good, man. My tires have been slashed... yep... Half Moon Hotel... don't worry about that, but I want to get this on record... yeah, send Willard out here, and I'm going to need a ride... ... *what?*... you're fucking kidding..." He glanced at her from the corner of his eye. "... okay... Hey, I need you to look into something for me. Might be a long shot, but... Alright, will do. Be careful out there. Bye."

"What's going on?" She asked when he disconnected.

He paused, keeping his gaze on his truck. "We're trapped on the mountain."

"What?"

"The river flooded and collapsed the bridge."

"You're freaking *kidding*."

"My words exactly. More or less."

She felt her pulse skyrocket. "You're joking."

"I wish, but no. They officially closed the mountain."

"Are you telling me there's only one way up the mountain, to this hotel?"

"Yep. And it's flooded."

"Wow. This is..." She laughed a humorless laugh and shook her head.

A moment of silence ticked by.

"So... What now?" She asked.

He nodded to the far side of his truck. "Park there."

"There's no spot."

"Sure there is; just park in the grass."

"On the edge of the woods?"

"Yep."

"I'd have to hop the curb."

He slid her a glance. "Need me to handle this for you, Miss Reece?"

She rolled her eyes, then carefully edged around his truck and bumped over the curb. Branches swiped the side of the vehicle—the *rental* car that he was paying for—but he didn't seem to care. She shoved it into park, pushed the emergency brake and turned to him.

"Wes, what are you doing here?"

"Well, I'm helping you park your vehicle."

"I mean, *here, here*. The hotel. You said you were following up on some things."

"That's right."

Gwen clicked her tongue and shook her head. "You're not telling me something, *again*, and I want to know what it is. Right now."

She stared at him as he continued to look forward. Finally, he said, "Leena was wearing a bracelet when I found her. A bracelet I got for her. Except when I looked closely, I noticed a small cross pendant on it, loosely tied on, that wasn't there when I got it for her."

He looked over at her and she tried to hide her surprise.

He continued, "I took it to a friend, a jeweler, who told me the green gemstone in the center of the cross is something called Chrome Diopside, only found in Russia. And she only knew of one place around here that sells jewelry with the gemstone."

"Here."

"Yep."

"Where your tires were just slashed."

"Yep."

"You think you were lured here."

"Yes."

"By Leena's murderer."

Wesley nodded. "He baited me. Killed her in my basement, put the pendant on the bracelet I got for her. He knew I'd find it, and it led me here."

"But why here... and *who*..." her voice trailed off.

Wesley paused and she knew there was much more to this story. Little did she know, how much.

"Do you remember the murders here, five years ago. Two young women—"

Her eyes rounded as she cut him off. "Taken from a hiking trail, drugged, tortured and eventually shot to death." A shiver swept over her arms. "Yeah, I remember. It was all over the news."

"Well, I had a hand in getting the guy who did it locked up."

"What do you mean *a hand?*"

He told her the story that happened at his sister's shooting range years ago.

She sat in silence for a moment, then said, "But why do you think he's associated with the cross?"

"Mikhail Lutrova is Russian. A proud Russian. Has the flag tattooed on his arm, even. Anyway, I spoke with the woman who runs the jewelry store downstairs, who told me that someone purchased a cross pendant with Diopside three days ago."

"*Three* days ago?"

"Yes."

"And Leena died two days ago."

Thunder boomed, rattling the windows. A chill tickled up her spine like fingertips tapping, warning her, pushing her to run. "Did the jewelry store owner tell you anything else?"

"No."

"Not even if it were a man or woman?"

"Nope."

Gwen chewed on her bottom lip. "He's still locked up, right?"

"For life, yeah."

"So... why do you feel so sure it's him. I mean, yeah, I see the Russia coincidence, but still..."

Wesley turned to her with an intensity that had her spine straightening.

"Because, Gwen, the day I called the cops on him was exactly five years ago, *today*."

"What?"

"Yeah."

"Today?"

"Yeah."

"But... he's locked up." Her voice pitched. "How the hell...?"

"I don't know. Could have someone else doing this for him. I don't know."

"Someone else delivering his revenge?"

"Your guess is as good as mine at this point. So there you have it. There's your story. That's why I'm here."

"You've got to tell Dean."

"I will. I just tried to tell him, but he got a call about a body found and had to go. Probably someone drowned in this damn rain."

"Okay." She took a deep breath. "Thank you for telling me."

Another boom of thunder shook the windows.

Gwen leaned forward, looked up at the sky. "So what do we do now?"

"Stay here, lock the door. I'll be right back." Wesley slid the red plaid button-up over his T-shirt to conceal his gun.

"Wait, what're..." But it was too late, he was out the door and jogging up the hill. She locked the door and watched in the rearview mirror as he disappeared around the side of the hotel. Seconds later, he emerged in a covered golf cart. A grin spread across her face. It might not have been an overcoat over a puddle, but definitely just as romantic. Possibly, more so.

He stopped at the back of the SUV and nodded for her to get in.

Gwen swallowed the grin, got out and jumped into the cart. Sideways rain whipped inside as they started up the hill.

"How did you know this was there?"

"Noticed it when I parked. Lucked out that the keys were in it. Sorry there's no side cover."

"Are you kidding? We'd be swimming without this thing. Thank you. But you could have just taken me to the front door, then parked the car yourself. If you were going to go to this much trouble anyway."

He hesitated. "I just want to get my head around what's going on before..."

"Before what?"

"Before I let you out of my sight."

The implication of the statement had a lump forming in her throat. "Do you think *I'm* in trouble?"

"No, but you've been seen with me. Whoever slashed my tires saw us talking."

Wesley pulled under the circle drive and stopped at the steps.

"But, that doesn't necessarily—"

He cut her off, turned fully toward her. "How do you feel about going to the ball tonight?"

Her eyebrows shot up as she realized he was serious. "Uh... *no*. I'm not exactly in a party mood."

"It's not to party."

And then she got it. Whoever was out to get Wesley would possibly be at the ball later.

"I see." She looked down. "Well, I don't think my hiking boots are appropriate attire..."

"We'll get you a dress downstairs."

"Uh, well, I don't dance, Wes."

He smiled, a twinkle in his eye. "Everyone dances."

"Says who?"

"Says me. Just takes breaking out of that shell of yours a bit." He tapped her arm. "No pun intended."

"Shell... bugs, I get it." She chewed her lower lip but before she could come up with another excuse, he hopped out of the cart, walked around to her side and held out his hand. He leaned in and whispered. "Don't mention what just happened to anyone. Just act like everything's cool, okay?"

She nodded, clasped his hand and despite the unease brewing in her belly, got out of the golf cart and tried her best to act "cool."

As they walked around the cart, a red pickup in the distance snagged Wesley's attention. The running lights glowed through the blur of rain, and she could just barely make out the dark silhouette behind the steering wheel.

Wesley cleared his throat, snapping her attention back to him. He smiled a casual smile. "Shall we?"

He was minimizing what was happening around them—for her. So she wouldn't worry. Wouldn't be upset. Or scared. But she knew it was all a show.

After a quick inhale, a mental thump on the chest, Gwen nodded and fell into step with him up the stairs. They pushed through the front door as two, drunk, giggling girls stepped off the elevator. The blonde, wearing a skin-tight sweater, mini-skirt, and bright red cowboy boots stopped laughing immediately when she saw Wesley. Her eyes narrowed, her lip curled to a snarl. Then, she looked at Gwen, giving her an ice-cold stare before looking back at Wesley. The pissed-off cowgirl squared her shoulders and stomped across the room, with the other close on her heels.

"Who's this?" The blonde demanded, addressing Wesley.

"I'm Gwyneth Reece," she answered for Wesley. "You are?"

The blonde narrowed her eyes. "Kaylee Rhodes, and this here's Lydia Hess." She looked Gwen over. "Don't believe we've met."

"No, we haven't." Gwen narrowed her eyes. "I'm sure I'd remember those boots."

Wesley grinned beside her as Kaylee looked down at her feet, trying to decide if Gwen had just delivered a compliment or an insult.

Before the girl's head exploded, Gwen said, "I'm not from here. From Austin."

"Oh really?" Kaylee looked at Wesley. "Dipping your toes in different area codes? What happened, all dried up here in Berry Springs?"

"Kaylee," Wesley said, cool, calm and collected. "I think it's time to be on your way."

Lydia grabbed Kaylee's arm. "He's right. Sam's supposed to meet us at the bar."

A devilish smirk crossed Kaylee's face. "You remember Sam, right? Was my roommate for a while." Still addressing

Wesley, she looked at Gwen and said, "You met her when you picked me up for our first date." She paused. "I used to date your little boyfriend here. Before he started seeking out foreigners."

Gwen cocked a brow and meeting the blonde's wicked tone said, "He's not my boyfriend, and if you consider Austin, Texas, foreign, I need to get you a map."

Wesley laughed as Lydia dragged Kaylee away.

"If those are the kind of women you date, I can certainly see why you're still single."

"I was young and dumb."

"Yeah, she's hell on wheels." Gwen shook off the icy interaction, then looked around, taking a mental image of every face. Every face belonging to someone who could've slashed Wesley's tires. Every face, someone who could have killed Leena Ross.

Melanie sat behind the reception desk, texting on her cell phone. In the corner of the lobby, a woman with wild, curly black hair in a fitted maid's uniform—unbuttoned just enough to see her voluptuous cleavage—mopped up shoe prints from the shiny hardwood floors. She looked up and zeroed in on Wesley, and instantly, a small, shy smile crossed her lips before she quickly looked back down. Gwen rolled her eyes. The bickering couple they'd passed on their way out stood impatiently next to the elevator, the wife wiping her designer jacket with a sour expression on her face. The man, also dressed in an expensive-looking suit, rested his hand on a cart packed with four bags of matching luggage, a logo she'd seen in the latest issue of Vogue. An older man in a golf cap sat reading the newspaper, and she noted that James, the bellman, was nowhere in sight.

Wesley, who had been scanning the faces as well, grabbed her hand and led her to the front desk.

Melanie looked up from her phone. "Hi, again." She smiled at Wesley, then frowned. "Oh my God, you're soaked."

So was Gwen, but of course the girl didn't notice.

"Hey, do you know where the bellman is? James?"

Melanie glanced at the front door. "Oh, um, I think he's on his dinner break. He'll be back soon. Can I help you with something?"

Wesley tossed the golf cart keys on the counter. "No, I just borrowed this. Wanted to return it. What's James's last name again?"

"O'Connor."

"That's right. One more thing. You mentioned there aren't very many people staying here this evening?"

"Right." She clicked a few keys on the computer. "Just the staff, a *thin* staff tonight, and... eight others, excluding your friend." She glanced at Gwen.

"Thanks, Melanie."

"No problem." Her gaze trailed down to Wesley's muscular chest, outlined by his drenched T-shirt, which Gwen had already noticed. "Do you need a towel or anything?"

"Naw, I'm good."

"Okay. The maid, Elise, can get those clothes washed for you. Do you want me to call her up?"

"No, thanks."

"Okay, then." She smiled. "You really should consider the ball tonight."

"You know, I think we might."

"Great. I hope to see you there, then."

"Thanks, Mel." He turned from the counter and grabbed Gwen's hand. His grip was firm and commanding, and a mix of emotions had her brain fogging. She was trapped on the top of a mountain in a creepy hotel during a raging thunderstorm, quite possibly with a murderer lurking in the shadows. But she was trapped with *him,* with Wesley Cross, who gave her butterflies every time he touched her. Every time he looked into her eyes. Hell, every time he said her name.

At that moment, she realized that even with everything unfolding around them, she felt safe. *With him.*

Wesley guided her across the lobby, keeping her hand close to his hip. She glanced up at him, thoughts jumbling in her head. He looked down at her and the tight expression on his face softened.

He smiled. "Let's get you that dress, Gwen."

15

THIRTY MINUTES, TWO glasses of Champagne, and one black velvet dress later, Gwen stood on a red-carpeted raised platform encircled with mirrors, gazing at the reflection staring back at her. Her eyes widened.

"Bellissima." The owner of the dress shop and part-time makeup artist, Sally, smiled, obviously pleased with her creation. And creation it was. Gwen almost didn't recognize herself.

She knew she was in good hands the moment she met Sally, who was impeccably dressed in a fitted navy-blue suit, with a bevy of jewels around her neck. Her hair was pulled back in a slick bun, not a strand of hair out of place, and her makeup flawless. The artist had taken Gwen's limp, frizzy hair and created beachy waves that ran down her back. She'd braided the sides, intertwining little white flowers, and clipped them back, creating a crown-like effect. Gwen's eyes were dark and lined, the "smoky eye" as Sally had called it, and her lips a pale shiny pink that matched the blush dusted along her cheekbone. She felt... like a princess. Beautiful. Confident.

The dress—*the gown*—had a black velvet bodice that faded to gold silk chiffon at the waist and draped like water against her legs. When she saw it on the rack, she knew instantly it was the one. It reminded her of the women in the black and white pictures that hung throughout the hotel. As she looked back at herself now, she looked just like one of them.

Old-world glamour, she thought as she sipped her Champagne from a stemmed glass, which had magically appeared in her hand minutes after Wesley had pulled Sally aside and whispered something she couldn't hear. She guessed it went something like *here's my no-limit credit card, get this woman anything she wants.* She could see him saying something like that because that's what Wesley Cross did. He made demands in his flirty, charismatic way, and everyone fell in line. What a world this guy must live in, she'd thought. But she also knew he'd also said it because he wanted to make her happy, and that thought sent a tingle of excitement through her. He'd disappeared after ensuring Sally was capable, and the Champagne was cold.

"Almost done," Sally said as she grabbed a box from the floor.

"*Almost?* Sally, you've done an amazing job. What else…"

"You going barefoot, dear?"

Shoes.

Her eyes sparkled as Sally opened the box and carefully lifted a strappy, black shoe with a diamond-encrusted six-inch heel.

"Oh, my *God*, Sally."

The woman smiled. "I know. Christian Louboutin." She held them up, carefully turning them in her hands. "I ordered them from New York. I have dreams about these."

Together, they marveled at the shoe as if looking at the baby Jesus.

Sally continued, "You're a lucky girl, Gwyneth." She kneeled down, raised Gwen's foot and slipped it on.

Perfect fit.

Gwen looked down at her feet, now sparkling back at her.

Cinderella.

She smiled, and whispered, "Yeah, tonight, I am."

With that, Sally stood and stepped back. "I think you're ready for the ball, my dear." She placed her hand on the red curtain, "Shall we?"

Gwen took one last look in the mirror and nerves fluttered through her. She wanted to take a picture. She was sure she'd never look like this again, and she wanted to remember it. She wanted to remember the *feeling*.

Wesley sipped his beer and made his hundredth pass around the dress shop. What was it about women and getting ready? He'd grabbed the first tux and shoes that fit and was undressed and dressed in under three minutes. Why did women take so long? What the hell did they do in there? Not that he minded this particular delay much. He had an ice-cold beer and a chance to case the floor, the staff, and the people wandering it, which weren't many. Eight people staying in the hotel, plus staff. How much staff, he wondered? And who was in the hotel that hadn't reserved a room? He hadn't been able to get the odd conversation he'd had with the bellman, James, out of his head, and especially the fact that James wasn't at his post when they'd come back from discovering his tires flat. And who had the kid called seconds after he and Gwen had stepped away? It didn't sit well with him. He needed to know more about the kid. He pulled out his cell phone and scrolled down to Dean's number but paused. Dude was probably burning the candle at both ends, so he opened a new text to Officer Willard, instead.

You know anything about a James O'Connor? Young kid, bellman at Half Moon, and his dad, Trace O'Connor? Also can you check into Mikhail Lutrova? He's still in the state pen, right? Just verify.

He hit send and clicked through the rest of his messages. Nothing from Jessica, although he hadn't expected it. He knew DNA tests took time, but maybe, just maybe she'd uncovered something over the course of the afternoon. The bracelet should be easy enough to scan, but testing the blood on Leena's neck for two sets of DNA was a longshot. Then again, he'd built a career on longshots, and making them stick.

Wesley tucked his phone back into his pocket and ran his fingers over a red silk gown hanging on the wall, imagining Gwen's body underneath it. She'd look smokin' hot in it, or out of it, for that matter. He grinned, recalling the first time he'd seen her. Somehow, the woman had even made an over-sized lab coat look sexy.

He focused on the low cut of the dress and found himself wondering what she looked like naked. The blood funneled between his legs along with a rush of heat up his neck.

Jesus, Wes.

He cleared his throat, turned away and took a swig of beer. As much as he hated to admit it, Gwen was a bit of a mystery to him. She was tough, with just enough of an attitude to make a man have to work for it, but not so much to turn him off. She was independent and driven, too, working her ass off to build a career and a name for herself. But hands down, his favorite thing about her was that she was smart, which was something he wasn't accustomed to with the women he dated.

Was she smart enough to stay away from him, he wondered as a wave of insecurity swept over him.

Dean had informed him over coffee that the Caregiver Killer had been found earlier that day. Was it a coincidence the murderer was caught less than twenty-four hours after Gwen had been on the scene? No shot in hell. Gwen was good at what she did and dedicated, that much was evident. Her heart was in it one hundred percent, which made him wonder if she had anywhere else in her heart for a man. He wondered if having a relationship ever even entered her brain. He had a feeling if it did, it was a fleeting thought that she'd push away to refocus on work.

Gwen's career choice took balls, and that was sexy as hell to him. She spent her life analyzing bugs that dined on dead bodies. She used her finely-tuned skill set to help build a story of what had happened, help shape an investigation and get justice for the victim. Their lives weren't so different. Wesley had built a career hunting bad guys and delivering justice by capture... or kill. It wasn't for the faint of heart. It wasn't for the weak. And aside from his comrades, no one understood. No one understood the weight of the missions, or what it could do to a man to see the bodies of women and children brutally mutilated and murdered, or worse in some cases, mutilated, tortured and barely still alive, awake to see the massacre around them. No one understood the emotional toll the job took, even though no one on his team would admit to it. But it was there, buried deep down only to manifest itself in nightmares, stealing the only few hours of escape they were given in a day filled with hell. He'd seen counselors, psychologists, numbers of head doctors. Not because he wanted to but because he'd been ordered to. They all said the same thing: he needed to talk. Vent. They said it wasn't healthy to see the things he'd seen, and do the things he'd done, and not let it out. Some restless nights, he thought maybe they were right.

The girls he dated asked plenty of questions; wanted to hear all the stories. They didn't want to get to know *him*, to understand *him*. They simply wanted to put themselves in the television shows, the movies, into the fantasy of the danger and the heroes who eliminated that danger. With every girl, he'd felt like there was an entire side of him they never knew. A dark side. But he knew they didn't want to know that side, they only wanted to hear the heroic tales, followed by how much he could bench press.

His counselor said he should talk to someone in the same field. Someone with a similar lifestyle that would understand. Someone with an open heart and sympathetic ear.

Someone like Gwen.

He'd never met a woman that he thought, maybe—*maybe*—could understand him. The *real* him.

Could Gwen?

Wesley's attention shifted to movement across the room. He turned as the red curtain was pulled back.

And his heart fell to his feet.

For the first time in his life, he was speechless. Absolutely, totally, cat-got-your-tongue speechless.

Holy. *Shit.*

Gwen smiled, and all he could do was smile back. She was the most beautiful thing he'd ever seen in his life.

Sally grinned.

He cleared his throat and forced his legs to move forward. He took Gwen's empty champagne glass, set it on the counter, and with his eyes locked on hers, kissed the back of her hand.

Her cheeks reddened.

"You're... absolutely beautiful."

"Thank you," she beamed.

"Shall we?"

Gwen turned to Sally. "Thank you, Sally. For everything."

"You're welcome, dear. Now go." She patted her backside. "Go. Have a good time."

He helped her off the platform and as Sally walked away —to the cash register he assumed—Gwen said, "Thank you, Wes."

The smile on her face and the sparkle in her eyes was worth every second he'd stood waiting on her. She was so happy, and that made him feel like a million bucks.

With her hand in his, Wesley led Gwen out of the shop and down the hall, and noticed he stood a little straighter with her by his side.

That is, until she stumbled.

As he steadied her, she burst out laughing. A belly-laugh that seemed to light the whole hallway. And that did it. He pulled her to him, her face inches from his. The moment her big, brown eyes met his, his heart skipped a beat. He realized then that he was powerless against them. Against her. Those eyes, those full, pink lips. God, he wanted her. He wanted to take her to her room, rip off the dress that probably cost him the revenue of three guns and have his way with her until she couldn't scream his name one more time.

Her eyes flared with heat as if she'd just read his thoughts. But just as quickly, she pulled back, her cheeks flushed.

"Sorry." Gwen laughed softly. "I'm not used to these shoes. I don't really get into heels much."

Cold air replaced the heat between them. He slid his hand over hers. "I guess you'll have to hold on to me all night, then."

"I can handle that."

He led her up the stairs—nimble on his feet this time—and down a dim hall that ended at a massive set of French doors. Beyond the beveled glass, candlelight twinkled. A low, melancholy tune floated through the air. A small dance floor centered the room with tables covered in black linen and fresh flowers positioned around it. Stained-glass windows, black with weather, lined the walls. Two chandeliers hung from the beams high above them.

"Drinks," Gwen demanded before he could scan the room. The tone in her voice and unease in her face told him the laughing, carefree woman from seconds earlier was gone.

This time, *she* led *him* across the room to a small bar in the corner.

16

THE BALLROOM OOZED a sort of gothic romance, with shadows from the candlelight dancing like ghosts along the walls. Under normal circumstances, it would be the most romantic evening Gwen had ever had. She'd make herself relax and loosen up and allow Wesley to take her onto the dance floor where she had no doubt he'd be the best dancer in the room. Because that was Wesley, good at everything.

But they were not under normal circumstances. Her Cinderella moment had momentarily pulled her from reality, but the second they'd walked into the ballroom, she'd felt like she had a target on her back.

Like someone was watching her.

She pulled Wesley to the bar, not just because she needed another drink but because it was in the corner, allowing for a full view of the room. In her quick scan, only a few people had decided to attend the ball. Good, fewer people to analyze.

"Howdy, there. Hell of a storm, isn't it?" The tall, salt-and-pepper haired bartender wiped his hands on a towel as he walked over. He wore all black, from the shiny dress shoes on his feet to the black tie, and black button-up. He was handsome, Gwen noticed, with sparkling blue eyes, and smooth tanned skin. He laid two napkins on the bar. "What can I get y'all?"

Wesley pulled out the leather stool for her and said, "I'll take a Shiner."

"Tap or bottle?"

"Bottle." He settled in next to her.

"And for you, ma'am?"

Gwen skimmed the liquor bottles lining the mirrored back wall. Beer wasn't going to cut it. "Rum and coke, please."

"You got it." The bartender walked away.

She cast a glance over her shoulder.

"You're safe, Gwen. You're safe with me," Wesley whispered in her ear.

Her eyes met his.

"I won't let anything happen to you."

Her heart fluttered as she looked back at him, all dressed up in his tuxedo, the sexiest version of James Bond she'd ever seen. His gaze so penetrating, so confident, so serious, that she absolutely believed him.

The bartender brought their drinks and laid a few menus on the bar. Gwen took a deep gulp, then picked up the menu and scanned the selection, although her brain wasn't registering the words. She had to fight the urge to glance over her shoulder again. This was ridiculous. Undercover work was for beautiful women who secretly knew martial arts and how to dismantle a pistol. She didn't. On both counts. She gave up, slammed down the menu and looked at Wesley.

"I just need to..." Gwen shook her head trying to piece

together her racing thoughts into coherent sentences. "We need to recap here. Okay, so five years ago *today*, you met Mikhail Lutrova, the Russian devil's spawn, who brutally murdered two women. That confrontation ultimately led to him getting locked up for the rest of his life."

"Right."

"And two days ago, your former lover was murdered in your basement, wearing a bracelet that you got her, which had a mysterious Russian pendant attached, which led you *here*, where your tires were slashed, ensuring that you couldn't leave."

"Righto." He tipped up his bottle and took a swig.

"Shit, Wes." She glanced at his jacket. "Do you still have your—"

"Of course. Clipped to my belt. Loaded."

Gwen released an exhale, then said, "We're crazy to not think it's the same person. But it can't be. Right? Mikhail's in prison, for life. Wait... could he have gotten parole?"

"Life without parole."

"Then it can't be him. It's someone else. Someone *here*." She felt herself coming unglued.

"Just calm down. Drink."

Her eyes darted around the dark ballroom and paused on the man in a golf cap swaying back and forth with his wife on the dance floor, and just behind them, a solo man in a cowboy hat seated in the far corner, shaded by shadows. The candlelight from a nearby table sparkled off the metal tip of his cowboy boots.

She leaned in and whispered, "Hey, did you notice—"

"The cowboy in the corner with a Stetson and steel-toed boots? Yes, I did."

"He's alone."

"Yes, he is."

"That's Bruce Jepsen." The bartender, apparently eaves-dropping, walked over. "Comes in here a lot, big hunter. Lots of deer in these mountains."

"Did you say hunter?" Gwen asked.

"Yep. Got him a sixteen-point last season. He's kind of legendary 'round here."

"From here?" Wesley kept his gaze on the man in the corner.

"Don't think so. Got a mansion, so they say, somewhere in Newton County. Kills all the deer over there, then makes his way here. Or so they say."

"He alone?"

"No. Brought a buddy with him this time."

"Where's he?"

The bartender looked out the windows. "Not sure, but definitely not hunting in this damn storm. Supposed to continue all night."

"What's he drive? You know?"

"Red truck, I think." He cocked his head, narrowed his eyes. "Why you askin'?"

"Just like to know who I'm trapped in the hotel with, Mr. ..."

"Beckham. Becks for short."

"Becks, then." He stretched out his hand. "Wesley Cross and this is Gwyneth Reece."

"Pleasure to meet y'all. And yeah, we're stuck. 'Least 'till morning, probably. The river will go down quickly."

"But they've got to repair the bridge," Gwen said.

"They'll get it done."

"There's really no other way off this mountain?" She asked.

"Nope. Only one road. Too rugged on the other side." He nodded toward Bruce Jepsen in the corner. "Great for huntin'."

"You a big hunter?" Wesley leaned forward.

"Naw, more into fishing, myself."

"Me, too." Wesley sipped, then said, "You catch and release or fry 'em up?"

Becks wiped a glass and lifted it, examining it under the dim light. "Filet and fry when the mood strikes me. Are y'all planning to order something to eat or just drinks?"

Wesley stared at him for a moment, then picked up his menu. "We'll eat. I'll take a cheeseburger and fries."

Gwen glanced down at the menu and recited the first thing she saw. "Turkey wrap, potato chips, please."

"You got it." He scribbled on a notebook and stepped away.

Gwen leaned in and whispered, "Ol' hunter Bruce Jepsen's got a buddy with him... you think it's the same guy watching us from the truck after your tires were slashed?"

Wesley nodded, sipped his beer. "Be my guess. I'd like to know what kind of knives they both carry."

Kaylee stumbled down the hallway, and a hiccup caught her.

Geez, how many drinks had she had today?

God, she was bored.

Why had Lydia waited so long to get dressed for the ball, anyway? It had been twenty minutes since she'd gone to her room to change clothes. Probably into some boring, gray cotton turtleneck and ill-fitting skirt that hung past her knees. She liked the girl, but *God*, she could stand to loosen up. She doubted Lydia had ever had a one-night stand in her life, and that's exactly what Lydia needed. A one-night stand—a proper send-off of her single years, days before she walked down the aisle. Yep, that's exactly what that girl needed. Maybe she'd lend her one of the five cocktail dresses she'd packed. Maybe the tight, red little number, or, no, the blue lace one to go with her eyes. Her *boring* eyes.

She glanced at her watch and cursed Sam. They still hadn't heard from her, but knowing Sam, she probably wasn't even going to show up.

Whatever, they'd have fun without that flakey wallflower anyway.

Kaylee stepped into the fourth-floor bar and looked around. Where the hell was everybody? When she'd booked the hotel for Lydia's bachelorette party, she hadn't realized most of the hotel was closed off for renovations. Who was she supposed to get drunk and make bad decisions with after boring Lydia and Sam went to bed?

Definitely not Wesley Cross, that's for sure.

Asshole.

She was shocked when she'd seen him in the lobby, but even more shocked when she saw him with a mystery woman later. Who was she? What did she do? Where did he find her? She was definitely prettier than her, right? She took a deep breath and shook her head. Wesley would find a reason to dump the little brunette, just like he did every other woman he dated.

Dated. Ha!

He'd probably leave the chick at the bar... and then maybe she'd find out his room number and sneak up. The thought had her cheeks flushing. Wesley Cross was just as hot as he was an asshole.

But, finding the asshole was not why she'd made her way up to the fourth-floor bar.

No, she had a bone to pick with someone else. She

wanted to know why the hell the FBI showed up at her doorstep earlier and more importantly, what Lawrence had to do with it.

She glanced at the clock on the wall—9:44. Fourteen minutes past the arranged meeting time. Where the hell was he? She skimmed the unmanned bar, cocked an eyebrow, and after taking a quick glance over her shoulder, jumped behind and yanked a beer from the cooler.

Don't mind if I do, she thought.

With a smirk, she decided to take her free drink out on the balcony and watch the storm.

Kaylee stepped outside, careful to keep her heels out of the cracks in the wood planks. The rain poured off the roof, just a few feet ahead of her. Lightning lit the mountains, and her stomach flopped as she realized how high she was. She took a sip.

A minute passed.

She took another sip.

A chill slid up her spine.

She pulled the bottle away from her lips, her body tensing from head to toe. She hadn't heard Lawrence walk up behind her, but there was no doubt she wasn't alone anymore.

She slowly turned, and instinctively took a step back.

"Wait. Who're you?"

17

"*A*H, HERE'S YOUR food now," Becks nodded behind them.

Wesley turned to see a tall, bulky man in a white chef's coat holding two steaming plates. His long hair was tied back and a thin, black necklace with a line of white teeth hugged his neck. A faint smell of cigarette smoke scented his arm as he slid the plates in front of them.

"Sorry it took so long. I'm the only one here." His voice was deep, gruff.

"No problem at all." Wesley nodded to the necklace. "Sharks teeth?"

"Coon."

"Coon, huh?"

"Yep. Dime a dozen 'round here. Mean. Smart. Cunning. Don't take crap from anyone. Reminds me to be the same."

"Mean and cunning?"

The man grinned. "No, smart, and no bullshit. Cunning when it suits me."

Becks walked up. "Thanks, Lawrence. They got you pullin' a double tonight, huh? Cooking and waiting tables?"

"Yep. Just me. They closed the mountain before Don could come in for his shift. Enjoy your food."

The cook walked away, and Wesley turned his attention to Becks. "Hey, what do you know about James O'Conner?"

"The bellman?"

"Yeah."

"Good kid." He wiped the bar top. "Been a bit off today, though."

"Off?"

"Guess he knew that girl that was killed. Y'all heard about it? Throat slit in someone's basement. Horrible."

Wesley shifted in his seat. "I heard."

Gwen leaned forward. "How well did he know her?"

"Not sure. Don't really talk much. Anyway, enjoy, and let me know if you need anything."

"Thanks."

"Well that's interesting," Gwen said as he walked away.

Wesley nodded. It *was* interesting, and now, more than ever, he wanted to know who the hell James called on the phone moments after they'd met.

"I wonder how good of friends," she continued.

"Willard'll find out."

"Maybe the kid was jealous of you, or thinks you had something to do with it?"

"And slit my tires because of it?"

She shrugged. "Yeah. He's young, at that 'invincible' age... fits if you ask me. You don't remember selling a gun to his dad?"

"Vaguely. I'd have to look at my records. I sell lots of guns, Gwen."

She stared down at her plate.

"Eat." He demanded. Dinner meant normal, and full stomach meant less emotional.

"*Mmph.*" She shrugged.

"Look, we're stuck here, and that's that. It sucks, but nothing we can do about it. Might as well eat dinner."

"If it's not poisoned," she muttered.

He grabbed her turkey wrap, took a bite, swallowed. "Still alive. Eat."

She took it from him. "Geez, alligator mouth."

"Alligator mouth?"

She held up the wrap. "Look how much you took. Half the wrap in one bite."

"Still... alligator mouth? Not very creative."

"Sorry, I'm not exactly on my A-game right now."

"I mean, sure, alligators have big mouths, but certainly not the biggest. Hippos for one... I'm pretty sure hippos can eat an alligator."

"Fine, hippo mouth, then."

"Or, mammoth mouth, maybe. Flows better."

Gwen picked up her butter knife. "I'm going to stick this into your alligator mouth if you don't shut up."

"Does it have to be a butter knife?" He leaned in and whispered. "'Cause I've got a few other ideas..."

The sound of a muffled argument behind them drew their attention.

The designer husband and wife, dressed to the nines, were at it again. Wearing a lacy black number, the wife hissed at the husband, "I told you we shouldn't have come to this hell hole, and that goddamn storms were coming. I fucking hate the south. May the whole bottom half of the country burn in hell for all I care. I should've stayed home. Let you bring along your little *mistress.*"

As the bickering couple stepped up to the bar, Wesley glanced at Gwen who seemed amused at the wife's rant... until they sat down next to her.

He grinned and winked, then looked the couple over. By the swirly look in the woman's eyes, she wasn't only pissed off, but apparently drunk—a lethal combination in any man's book. Botox and fillers aside, the woman appeared to be half her husband's age, with *gold digger* stamped on her wrinkle-free forehead. The man, a business man on all counts, sported slicked-back hair, a three-piece suit with personalized gold cuffs. He ordered a scotch on the rocks and, what else, a glass of champagne for his brooding wife.

"Good evening." The man addressed them as if he didn't have a care in the world.

The woman snorted and slurred, "Good evening, my ass."

"Evening," Wesley slid his arm on the back of Gwen's chair, claiming his territory. He leaned forward as Gwen leaned back, sending him a nonverbal message for him to run the conversation. His pleasure.

"Beautiful place." The man said.

"It is."

"Are you from here?" He asked Wesley.

"Born and raised."

The wife rolled her eyes at this.

"My name is Cortez Vega, and this is my wife Amelia."

Amelia leaned forward. "Charmed, I'm sure." She looked Gwen over, her pointy eyebrows tipping up. "Nice dress. Valentino?"

Gwen shrugged, and Wesley grinned at her lack of knowledge of designer duds. Forget smart, that was officially one of his favorite things about her now.

"Well." Amelia followed the compliment with, "I don't know why the hell anyone would want to live here. Dirty South, it truly is."

Cortez shook his head and leaned forward trying to

block his wife as Becks delivered their drinks. Amelia swept back her platinum blonde hair and took a sip, pinky raised.

"Wesley Cross," they shook hands. "And this is Gwyneth Reece."

"You'll have to excuse my wife." His gaze lingered on Gwen a moment too long. "We've had a long day of travel, with the weather and all."

Feeling a surprising rush of protectiveness, Wesley slid his hand from the chair onto Gwen's back, lightly rubbing his thumb on her shoulder. She felt good. The touch, the connection. He liked it. He liked touching her, intimately, as if she were his. She turned to him, eyes bright at his intimate touch and stared at him for a moment.

God, she was beautiful. He smiled, the urge to kiss her slowly leaning him forward. This was met with the turn of her cheek, so he swallowed that rejection like a bowling ball and addressed the miserable husband.

"What brings you to Berry Springs?"

"Business. I'm looking at buying some land in the area."

"Where about?"

"Along the river. Considering putting in a resort. There's so much tourism here."

"A resort... wait, did you say your last name was Vega?"

"Yes. I own the Vega hotel chain. You know it?"

Everyone knew the name. The luxurious hotels were speckled all over the world, all very exclusive, and all five-star.

"Yes, I know the hotels." He paused, took a shot in the dark. "I visited one in Russia once."

"Really? What took you there?"

"Work," he said.

"And what business are you in, Mr. Cross?"

"I make guns."

"Guns?" Amelia leaned forward, her eyes round. "Do you happen to have one on you now to put me out of my misery?"

"Would be too quick," her husband said icily, while keeping his eyes on Wesley.

Wesley tightened his grip around Gwen's shoulder.

"Screw you," Amelia muttered, then flagged down the bartender. "Another glass."

"Yes, ma'am." Becks grabbed a fresh glass and poured her drink. In a huff, she pushed out of her chair—spilling half the Champagne onto the bar and said, "You guys enjoy your evening. I'm going to go find something better to do with my time."

As Wesley watched her saunter into the lobby, his gaze shifted to the corner of the room. The cowboy in the Stetson and steel-toed boots was gone.

Cortez grabbed his drink and stood. "I probably should go after my wife. Would be a pity if she tumbled over the fourth-floor balcony."

Gwen raised her eyebrows.

"Have a good night."

Wesley and Gwen exchanged a glance just as his phone rang.

He snatched it up. "Cross here."

"Cross, it's Steele. I hope you're sitting down."

He cut a glance at Gwen and considered stepping away for the call. But, no; he didn't want to leave her alone. "Hey, Gage. What'd you find out?"

"I got you Mikhail Lutrova's file, it's in your inbox. But I'm assuming you haven't been watching the news this afternoon?"

"No, been kinda busy."

"Thought so. Mikhail Lutrova broke out of prison three days ago."

His stomach fell to his feet. *"What?"*

"Yep. FBI's kept it quiet, until now. Spent the first full day chasing a false lead. They're combing the area now, but have no concrete leads, or so I was told."

"How did he—

"Wire cutters. Son of a bitch clipped one link at a time in one of the outside fences. No telling for how long. Got out and vanished."

"Where the hell did he get wire cutters?"

"Exactly. Had to have someone on the outside, who also possibly picked him up."

"Who's on the prison log recently?"

"No one."

The image of Mikhail Lutrova's evil, ice-blue eyes flashed in his head.

"Good chance he's changed his appearance by now, his identity, the works. Or is on a beach in Mexico somewhere."

"I don't think that's the case."

"For some reason, I didn't think you did. Care to fill me in here?"

Wesley looked at Gwen as he said, "Mikhail Lutrova isn't on a beach in Mexico, Steele, he caught a ride to the Half Moon Hotel in Berry Springs."

His pulse picked up as the shock spread over Gwen's face.

He needed to get her away, somewhere safe.

Immediately.

18

TREE BRANCHES SWIPED madly at the windows outside, the trees whirling in the angry wind. Vertical lightning sliced the sky like electric tentacles reaching out to get her. Then came the thunder, not a low bellow but a crackle, popping, startling her even though she expected it. Like bombs exploding in the distance.

Gwen squeezed Wesley's hand as he pulled her through the lobby. Seconds after his conversation with someone named Steele, he'd paid the tab and escorted her out of the ballroom. There had been a total shift in his demeanor. An urgency she hadn't seen before.

Mikhail Lutrova was here. The man who brutally murdered two young women, possibly three now, was here. And she was with the man who had a target on his back.

Her heart raced and she must've tightened her grip on Wesley's hand because he looked down at her, and smiled.

She didn't smile back.

He gave a slight nod—*you're okay*, it said.

She looked at the antique clock on the wall—11:17 p.m.—

and just below that, a man and woman stood in the shadows. She squeezed his hand and whispered, "Look..."

He kept his gaze straight ahead. "At Lydia whispering with James O'Connor? Already noticed."

Of course he did. The man could read an entire room without turning his head.

He led her to the front desk where Melanie stood, staring at the computer, her brow furrowed, her skin pale. Something was wrong.

"Melanie," Wesley said.

Startled, her eyes shot up from the computer. Bloodshot red over dark circles. She looked like a completely different person than when she'd checked Gwen into the hotel. "Sorry... yes? Hi. How can I help you?"

Wesley frowned. "You okay?"

"Yeah. Yes." Melanie clicked a few keys, and the screen went blank. "Just... didn't really plan on being stuck here tonight." She glanced out the windows.

He watched her for a moment and Gwen did, too. The weather wasn't the only thing wrong with this girl, that much was obvious.

"Anyway, how can I help you?"

"Considering none of us are going anywhere this evening, I need to get a room."

Melanie nodded and turned back to the computer.

"Next to Gwyneth Reece, please."

Wesley squeezed her hand as nerves skittered through her. He was getting a room *next to her*. Most women would probably be jumping out of their skin—or panties, for that matter—at the thought of sleeping less than twenty feet away from the incredibly sexy, handsome Wesley Cross. And those women had probably had sex within the last twelve months. Not her. Hell, she wasn't even sure if everything still worked down there. It had been almost a year since she'd had sex. The last time was with Ryan, three months before they'd officially ended their relationship. *Three months.* And it was horrible, forced, fake, emotionless. Anything but romantic. She'd even faked an orgasm just to move things along. After that night, she'd realized that was how their sex had been all along—*boring*. No heat, no passion, no animalistic lust. Just plain boring.

And that was her opinion of sex. Tragic, wasn't it.

"Is James back from his break?" Wesley said, shaking her from her racy thoughts.

"No, not yet. He gave me your girlfriend's bag to hold." Melanie pulled the bag around the corner of the desk. "I guess you'd dropped it off with him earlier."

Girlfriend.

Wesley took the bag, and Melanie handed him the key. "You both are on the fourth floor. End of the hall, adjoining rooms. I've included two complimentary drink tickets for the bar up there. The view from the balcony is breathtaking. Not that you'll be able to appreciate it with this storm and all."

"Thanks, Melanie."

"No problem."

As he grabbed her bag, Gwen whispered, "What now?"

"Hunker down."

Hunker down... in their *adjoined* rooms.

Oh, dear God.

Wesley carried her bag as they stepped into the rickety elevator that gave her the willies just looking at it. It appeared antique, like everything else in the hotel, and an *antique* elevator was the last thing she needed to calm her nerves. The small, suffocating box creaked as Wesley's over-two-hundred-pound body stepped onto it. Thank God she'd packed light. He hit the fourth-floor button, and with a jolt, the elevator began to slowly lift.

She looked at her reflection in the cracked mirror but was distracted by the man standing next to her. He was so damn handsome. Her gaze trailed from his arms, to his chest, to his face, where he watching her, scanning over him like a piece of meat. The look in his eyes caught her breath —the heat, the fire of it. There was no mistaking what was on his mind at that moment.

Her heart started to beat faster.

The elevator bumped, knocking her off balance and, true to form, he caught her. The inches closed between them. Despite everything telling her to keep her gaze ahead, she turned to him, her heart like a drum now. He reached up and cupped her face, stared at her for a moment before saying, "Relax, Gwen. Everything's going to be okay, alright?"

She nodded, unable to form a single sentence. Paralyzed by the flame in his eyes.

And then he did it. Wesley Cross pressed his lips to hers and butterflies exploded in her stomach, her knees turning to water.

Oh, my God.

He kissed her, moving over her lips as if knowing exactly what she wanted. *Needed.* It was as if he knew exactly how she kissed. As if they'd kissed a hundred times before. She felt a tingle between her legs as his other hand swept through her hair, to the back of her head.

Leaning into him, giving in to him, she wrapped her arms around his neck. At her nonverbal submission, his kiss intensified. His hands swept down to her ass as he backed her up against the wall, pressing his erection into her hip.

Then—*BOOM!*

The lights went out. The elevator jerked to a halt. Muffled shouts and yells sounded around them—not panicked, she noted immediately, not screams, but urgent voices nonetheless.

Gwen blinked, her eyes adjusting to the pitch-black darkness that surrounded her. She reached for Wesley.

"What the hell just happened?"

He grabbed her hand. "Power's out."

"No *freaking* way."

"Way."

"But the boom, the pop?"

"Lightning took out the power."

As he said it, she heard the howl of the wind whipping outside and the buzz of hail on the roof above them.

"Oh, my God. Wesley. We're in a freaking elevator!" Panic—claustrophobia—began to squeeze her chest. Being stuck in an elevator was officially one of her worst nightmares. *Oh, God,* did she need to pee?! She stilled for a moment, scanning her body. No. Okay, she was good there, praise the Lord.

A bright light suddenly filled the small space, and she squinted at the cell phone in his hand. They had light. She reached into her pocket.

"Wait... don't turn yours on. We need to conserve battery."

She froze. "Conserve battery? How long do you think we'll be stuck here?"

His lack of response was answer enough.

"Hold the light."

Gwen took the phone from him and watched as he tried to pry open the doors, with no luck.

"We're going to need something to pry it open. Do you have anything in your purse?"

She squatted down and searched through her bag. "A pen?"

He grinned, which surprisingly had an instant calming effect on her. "Don't think a pen is going to cut it."

She let out a sigh. "Then, no, that's all I have. You can't pry it open?" She sank onto the floor, the gold chiffon of her dress falling around her.

"No, this elevator is from the damn dark ages. We'll need someone to pry it open from the outside, and we'll crawl out. I'm going to yell, don't pee yourself."

She rolled her eyes. He called out several times, with no response. The muffled voices sounded at least a few floors down.

"Where do you think we are?"

"I'd say close to the fourth floor... although," he looked at her, a twinkle in his eye. "I'd kinda lost track of time."

I kinda lost track of myself, time, the universe, everything around me, she thought. She felt the heat begin to rise to her cheeks as he stared down at her, the corner of his lip curling up. She tore her eyes away. He'd just had his hands all over her ass and now they were stuck in an elevator.

Alone.

He turned and yelled out again.

A minute passed.

Tried one more time—nothing.

"We'll keep calling out." He clicked off the cell phone, and everything went dark.

A moment of silence, stillness, ticked by. The buzz of heavy rain drowned out the distant voices. Thunder boomed. She could feel the electricity in the air but wasn't sure if it was from the storm, or the sexual tension shooting between them.

The elevator creaked as he slid down next to her.

Another minute slid by.

"You okay?" He broke the silence, his voice low and soft.

"Yeah." She nodded, forgetting he couldn't see her through the darkness. Hell, she couldn't even see her hand in front of her face.

Another pause.

"With everything?" He asked.

The kiss, you mean.

"Yes," she whispered.

"Me, too."

Gwen stared into the blackness anticipating his touch, and when she felt his fingers lightly sweep up her arm, goosebumps erupted over her body. He pulled her to him. Her eyes desperately searched the inky air around them, wanting to look into his beautiful face, but instead, she found herself letting go. Allowing him to lead her in an erotic dance through the darkness. Every sense, excluding sight, was heightened. She smelled him—the musky scent of his skin. That all-male scent that drove her crazy. She listened to the soft sound of his breath, inhaling, exhaling as he drew her closer. She felt his fingertips on her face, and then she felt his lips on hers. The warmth of his mouth, the fireworks in her head as his lips slid over hers. Less soft and sensual this time, more passion, more heat. Everything else faded away, everything else except for an insatiable hunger for the man next to her. A hunger she'd never felt before.

His hand swept up her velvet bodice, onto her breast. She arched like a feline.

Grab it. And he did, just before he reached around and slowly slid down the zipper. Her pulse skyrocketed as the fabric loosened around her and fell to her waist. She held her breath, waiting for his touch, and when he cupped her bare breasts, a shiver rushed over her. Her nipples perched at the touch, sending a shot of electricity up her spine. And that was it. She had to have him.

Right. Then.

She fumbled with his belt, sliding off his pants as he impatiently worked her dress down. Within seconds she had him undressed, her clothes were off, and she smiled at the freedom that came with the darkness. She didn't have to worry about a bloated stomach, the size of her breasts, or the few stubborn spots of cellulite on her butt. She was free to just be who she was, and with that thought, an unexpected confidence took over her. She got onto her knees and pressed his back against the wall, pinning him. She worked her way between his legs and leaned into his neck, licking, sucking, nipping, while pressing her breasts against him.

He tipped his head back and groaned.

She took his erection in her hand, squeezed and stroked as she licked her way down his chest, down his rippled six-pack, and finally between his legs. He sucked in a breath as she tasted him, filling her mouth.

"*Fuck*, Gwen," He breathed, as she slid back and forth. He squirmed, then gripped her and pulled her to him. His lips crushed into hers as she crawled over him, straddling him, spreading her legs widely, hovering above his rock-hard cock. He cupped her ass, firmly, pressing her against him. His face was on her neck now, kissing, kissing, kissing.

She leaned back as he swept a hand between her legs.

"Touch me," she whispered.

Before she could take another breath, he slid a finger into her, and another, then rubbed the wetness over her clit, tiny, soft circles over the sensitive bud. Tingles flew over her skin. She gasped for air as he pressed harder, rubbed faster. Her head swam with the euphoric sensation taking over her body, the heat building and building between her legs. She rocked against him, unable to contain the energy coursing through her veins.

She couldn't control it.

She didn't want to.

"*Wesley.*" His name screamed from her lips as the orgasm sliced through her.

The waves of pleasure had barely stopped when he gripped her waist, positioned her over him and speared into her. Her breath caught as he filled every inch of her, stretching her to places she'd never felt before.

And it felt good. Damn good. Sated, dazed, she relaxed onto him, opening the river of wetness to him.

"God, *Gwen.*" He whispered as he pumped into her, his hands gripping her hips so tightly she felt his nails pressing into her skin. She rode him, hard, the friction against her clit driving the daze of her first orgasm away. Sweat beaded over her body, and his, too. Chests heaving, gulping for air, moving together, their sweat-slicked skin enhancing every sensation.

She felt him tense beneath her, and she knew he was close. She bucked, ground against him, the tingles burning, moving toward another explosion.

Her breath stopped. Body trembled.

And then she released, for the second time, as his hot liquid filled her up at the same time.

Breathless, she rested her forehead on his shoulder, an anchor, pulling her back to earth. *Oh. My. God.* were the only three words her brain could work up. His fingers slowly trailed her back as they caught their breath, together.

He kissed her head, then lightly tipped up her chin, and kissed her again. A smile caught her, then she slithered off him and collapsed on the floor.

He laid his hand over hers and took a deep breath. Although it was dark as coal, she felt him staring at her.

"Stay with me tonight." He said.

She smiled. "Assuming we ever get out of this elevator."

"Yes, assuming." He tugged at her hand—*come here.*

"Wes, I'm a sweaty mess."

He leaned over, grabbed her face and kissed her cheek. "I like it."

"*Stop.*" She laughed as she pulled on her panties—better than nothing. He did the same, into his boxers and pulled her to him, again. This time, she settled in the little nook between his arm and chest.

A few minutes passed.

She took a deep breath and closed her eyes. "I feel like a wet washcloth, dizzy, even."

"Adrenaline crash. Been a hell of a night."

"I don't think it's just an adrenaline crash." She smiled.

He kissed her forehead and lightly rubbed her arm. "My sister taught me yoga breathing. You ever tried it?"

"Ujjayi."

"You, what?"

She laughed. "That's what it's called. Ujjayi. And yes, I've done it many times. I take a hot yoga class when I'm in town. But I think it's going to take a lot more than Ujjayi breathing right now. Today's been... a lot."

"Which is exactly why you need to try to relax right now. We're safe." He chuckled. "Literally, *no one* can get us."

She looked up at him, through the darkness. "Do you always do this?"

"Do what?"

"Make light of shit situations so others won't worry. Carry the weight of it so others don't have to."

He paused for a moment. "There's a lot of bad in the

world. Genuine evil. I've seen it up close and personal. I guess... I want to shield people from that."

"I've seen it too, Wes." Her voice was low and soft.

He stilled next to her.

"Do you ever have nightmares?" She asked.

He paused and seemed to force himself to answer. "Some nights are worse than others."

"Same here. It drives me though, you know? Makes me work that much harder. Pushes me."

"I know exactly what you mean."

"I try not to make it personal. Not to get emotions involved, but it's tough. I do become invested, and when I'm able to help move an investigation forward, it just makes it all worth it. It's the best feeling in the world."

"But, before too long, it begins to define you. To take over." He said it as if he was saying it into the darkness. Words that have been locked inside of him, finally being released. "You are the mission, and nothing else. It completely takes over."

"Is that why you left?"

Another pause. "Yes. I wanted to make another life for myself."

"And you've done it, and based on the gossip I've heard, you've done a damn fine job of it." She lightly grabbed his hand. "But it still defines you, doesn't it? Deep down?"

She heard him swallow deeply.

"Don't let it."

He took a breath and kissed the top of her head. "Doesn't feel that easy sometimes."

She kissed the top of his hand. "For what it's worth, you can always call me. Middle of the night when you can't sleep, whatever. I guarantee you, I'm either hovered over case files of murdered bodies or having nightmares of one. I'll always understand."

He squeezed her. "Dammit, Gwen."

"What?"

"You just came out of nowhere, you know that?" He kissed the crown of her head, again.

"Right back at you."

A few minutes slid by.

"Have you ever thought about slowing down, though?" He asked. "I left my job that was twenty-four-seven. You're still in yours."

She took a deep breath. "According to my mom, and the endless pints of Ben and Jerry's I eat on Saturday nights, yeah, I probably should slow down a bit. At least travel less."

"Allow time for other things in your life."

"Exactly."

"So that it doesn't define you."

"Touché." She nestled deeper into his chest. "Can I tell you a secret?"

"Does it involve me and a pair of fuzzy handcuffs?"

She laughed. "No."

"A naughty teacher costume? Or in your case, maybe a bug costume?"

She slapped his arm. "*No.*"

"Okay, fine. Go ahead."

"I'm thinking about taking some time off after this little adventure you've got me on."

"Yeah? I one hundred percent encourage that. Where to?"

"Hawaii."

He blew out a whistle. "One of the best places for some relaxing time off."

"You've been?"

"A few times. It's beautiful. You really should do it."

"If we ever get out of here."

"Yeah... might be a bit... "

"Don't say that. The electricity could come back on any second."

"Maybe," he said, but she knew he didn't believe it. The mountain was closed. Who was going to fix it?

He stroked her arm. "Try to get some sleep. I'll wake you if anything happens."

19

"*KAYLEE... KAAAYLEE?!*"

Wesley jerked awake.

"*Kaylee?*"

Gwen raised her head off his chest. He sat up and silently pulled on his pants and shoes. The shouts were close, either on the floor above or below them. Wesley picked up his gun and slid it into his waistband.

"*Kayleeeeeee?*"

"Who..." Gwen whispered.

"That's Lydia. The brunette you met with Kaylee earlier." Earlier, or yesterday... what the hell time was it? He pushed to his feet and clicked on his cell phone as Gwen pulled on her dress—4:17 a.m.

After Gwen had fallen asleep in his arms, he'd stayed awake, hypersensitive to all the creaks and groans of the old building around them and had decided there was a positive and a negative to their entrapment. The negative was that he couldn't hunt down the son of a bitch that slashed his tires, and Leena Ross's throat. The positive was that Gwen was safe. And after what had just happened between them, the stakes had been significantly raised. Everything had changed. As he'd felt the heavy rise and fall of her chest, her little body curled perfectly into his, an overwhelming *protectiveness* gripped him. Not only to keep her safe but to protect the romance now happening between them. From the moment he'd laid eyes on her, in her mad-scientist goggles and over-sized lab coat, she'd grabbed him. Pulled at him and didn't let go. Truth was, he'd wanted to have sex with her within the first five seconds of meeting her, but he never expected to feel the way he did after.

As she'd slept, his mind drifted to crazy daydreams of taking her to the park, to the movies, cooking her breakfast. Doing normal couple things. Taking her on that vacation to Hawaii. He'd fantasized about what he was going to do to her the next time he got her clothes off and had even considered waking her up for round two. But he'd let her sleep, while he planned out the next ten years of their lives. He'd smelled her hair, stroked her head, and thought of what he would do if anyone ever touched a single strand of that beautiful hair. He wouldn't allow it. Not now, not ever. No one was getting through those elevator doors without him allowing it. And with that comfort, sometime around two in the morning, he'd drifted to sleep.

Wesley slid his phone into his pocket, stepped to the doors and cupped his hands. "Lydia?"

Nothing.

"Lydia!" He repeated.

Footsteps pounded the floor. *"Hello?"*

"Lydia! In the elevator!"

The steps raced down the hall, stopping directly in front of them.

"Wesley?! Is that you?" The light of her flashlight bounced through the crack in the door.

"Yes. We're stuck. We need you to pry open the doors, okay?"

"You've been stuck the whole time?"

"Yep. You're going to need to find a tool. What floor are we on?"

"Almost to the fourth. Have you seen Kaylee?" Her voice pitched with panic and his stomach filled with dread.

"Last I saw her she was with you. We've been in here ever since. What's going on?"

"She's missing, Wesley." Lydia's voice quivered. "Since, like, nine o'clock. I can't find her anywhere." She began sobbing. "It's been *all night*, Wesley."

Gwen grabbed his arm.

"Okay, Lydia, you've got to get me out of here so I can help you look for her, okay? Listen to me. I'm going to tell you what to do, okay?"

"Okay." She sniffled.

"There's a utility closet at the end of the hall. See if there's something long and thin to use to pry the door open. Strong, metal."

A moment of silence ticked by. "Like what?"

"I think there's potted plants and shrubs on the balcony, I bet there's gardening tools or something in there. Look for a shovel. Something like that."

"Oh. Okay... I'll be right back." Her footsteps faded down the hall, and every instinct in Wesley's body surged to life. Something was wrong.

"Wes..."

"It's okay. We'll get out of here, and the sun will be up before you know it." He reached for her face and kissed her. "I'll get you out of here. It's okay."

"But, Kaylee... what if..."

"Found a shovel!" The footsteps returned.

"Good job. Now, wedge the end of the shovel in the crack and use the handle as leverage to pry it open."

"Okay!"

Wesley watched as the tip of the metal hit the door, about six inches from the crack. Then, again, the same distance from the bullseye on the opposite side of the crack. After one more miss, he guessed Lydia had spent the majority of her time "looking for Kaylee" at the bar.

Finally, the fourth strike hit, and after a few grunts, the crack gave. He shoved his fingers inside and ripped the door open. Her flashlight blinded him.

"Good job Lydia. Move your light a bit." She did, and he assessed the situation. They were exactly midway between the third and fourth floor, which meant he'd have to heave Gwen up on his shoulders and hoist her onto the floor. It also meant that if the electricity happened to turn on while he was doing so, she'd be crushed.

He turned to Gwen. "You weren't a cheerleader by chance, were you?"

She snorted, seemingly offended by the statement.

He smiled, then said, "Okay, you're going to have to climb up on my shoulders, then pull yourself up. Sound good?"

"In this dress?"

"Unless you want to go naked, which I'm totally cool with."

"For the sake of keeping Lydia's head from exploding, no." She grabbed her diamond-encrusted heels. "But I'm taking these with me."

"Don't blame you. Okay... and you need to do it quickly, okay? If the electricity comes back on..."

She slowly nodded, her eyes wide with understanding, and looped her purse on her shoulder.

"Okay." He spun on his heel and squatted down. "Let's do this."

He heard her take a deep breath before locking hands with him, hiking up her dress and slinging her legs over his shoulders. He stood. "Nice and quick. I'll catch you if you fall."

"Or my body parts if this thing starts up."

"Can I choose the parts?"

She slapped his head.

"On three. One, two, *three*."

Gwen lifted off him, and after a quick shove of her butt, was safely on the fourth floor.

Phew.

Wesley pulled himself up and quickly scanned the floor, noticing how quiet the hotel was. The storm must have subsided over the last few hours. Someone had placed a flashlight at both ends of the hall, which did a crap job of illuminating, but it was better than nothing. When he was confident they were alone, he turned to Lydia.

"Tell me what's going on."

Lydia held the light so it shined up her face, creating black shadows over her eyes and below her cheekbones. "Well, I went upstairs to change." The liquor was thick on her breath. "And not too long after that the lights went out. I guess you know that. Oh, my God, I can't believe you've been stuck in that thing all night. How *freaky*."

"Lydia, focus."

"Okay. Yeah. I was in the bar waiting on Kaylee and after the lights went out, Melanie, the front desk chick, told us all to gather in the lobby while they set out lights throughout the hotel. I guess they were worried about us falling, or whatever."

"They don't have a generator?"

"What's a generator?"

"Never mind. Everyone gathered in the lobby?"

She nodded.

"Was Kaylee there?"

"No."

"What time did you last see her?"

"Oh, I don't know... around nine or so."

"Did you check her room?"

"Yeah. She's not there."

"Okay. Can you tell me who gathered in the lobby? Faces, at least?"

Lydia thought for a moment. "I wasn't really paying attention."

"Okay. Go on, then."

"So, someone went to go lay these flashlights around the halls—

"Who?"

"Uh... James, I think."

"The bellman?"

"Yeah. Anyway, after a while, I started getting worried and went to look for her." She shook her head, despair pulling at her face. "I went to her room, checked the halls, outside, even. Then, I went back to the bar, and later, checked again. I've been doing that off and on all night. Told Melanie, and she's been helping look for her, too."

"Where else have you looked?"

"All the places I could muster up enough courage to go... this place is so *creepy*, Wesley. Oh and I've checked the bathrooms, too. Her car, even."

"Still here?"

"Yes. The only place I haven't been is downstairs."

"The basement."

Lydia nodded, then grabbed his arm. "Also, Sam never

came down to meet us. She sent a text earlier that she'd checked-in, and we were supposed to meet at the bar, but she never showed."

Sam. He tried to recall the first, and only time he'd met Kaylee and Lydia's friend. It was at Kaylee's apartment, years earlier. Kaylee had introduced them and the twenty-something with short brown hair had barely looked up from the book in her hand. He remembered she seemed shy. Soft-spoken.

"When was the last time you heard from her?"

"After she checked-in. Said she was going to unpack. I've texted her several times, with no response."

His gut clenched. There were potentially two missing women now, not one.

"You've got to help me find Kaylee."

"The basement has a jewelry shop, spa, and I think the kitchen is down there," Gwen added.

He nodded. Many—*many*—places to hide. His mind raced to pull together a plan to find the missing Kaylee and Sam, while somehow ensuring Gwen was safe, and the only way he could do that was to keep her at his side. Her and the drunk, mentally unstable Lydia.

"Lydia, hand me your flashlight. I want you both to stay close to me, close to each other. Don't let the other out of your sight. We'll take the stairs to the basement to check it out." He turned fully to Lydia to emphasize. "Do not leave Gwen's side, do you understand?"

Wide-eyed, she nodded.

"Okay let's go, and stay quiet. Not a word." He led them down the hallway, his head on a swivel. James had positioned the flashlights pointing toward the center of the hall, blinding him, making it impossible to see past the bright light. He squinted, keeping his ears tuned to any sound around him.

They reached the balcony bar, and he stopped. "Did you check the bar?"

Lydia nodded. "Of course. I mean, I glanced in. No one's in there, not even a bartender."

He looked in the bar, his gaze landing on an open door that led to the balcony. An *open* door. His instincts piqued.

"Stay here. Right here. I'm going to check the balcony."

Wesley stepped into the bar, pulled his gun and swept the flashlight across the room. Red paisley carpet ran underneath round tables and leather chairs. A small bar lined the left wall, a bathroom on the far side. A wall of windows looked out to the dark balcony.

He checked behind the bar top, the bathroom, then made his way to the opened door that led out to the balcony. The night was eerily quiet. A cool breeze swept past his skin and the hair on the back of his neck prickled. Sliding his finger around the trigger, he stepped outside. The rain had stopped, but drops trickled from the awning above. The river raged in the distance.

He swept the light across the deck, until he found what he was looking for.

Kaylee Rhodes's throat had been slashed ear-to-ear.

20

"**S**TAY THERE!" WESLEY ordered Gwen, who was frozen in the doorway, her mouth gaping open. "Dammit, I told you to stay in the hall."

He quickly stepped over to the gray, lifeless body on the deck. Kaylee's eyes were open, staring up at the sky as if the lids had been peeled away. Blood mixed with puddles of rain, snaking across the wooden slats and dripping off the side.

So much blood.

She lay on her back, one arm hanging off the balcony and the other at her side, her fist closed. Between her fingers, something silver flashed in the light. Wesley kneeled down and peered closer at the small cross pendant with a green stone in the middle. His blood ran cold.

Suddenly, a bone-chilling scream from below.

Wesley surged to his feet and looked over the balcony. A dark silhouette darted across the lawn below.

A woman.

He spun around to face Gwen, who was desperately

pushing Lydia away from the door. *"Stay here."* He said. "Do *not* move. Do not leave. I'll be back."

He turned and threw himself over the banister, landing with a *thud* on the third floor. He crossed the balcony in two swift steps, then jumped down to the next level, then the next, until his boots hit the saturated ground. He slipped through the mud, then took off like a rocket, sprinting across the grass, following the footprints in the mud. Fallen tree limbs and branches threatened to trip him with each step, the mud stealing his balance. Wesley slowed, concentrating on the tracks that were fading against the gravel of the parking lot, then caught a glimpse of light coming from the side of the hotel.

"Hey!" He called out and sprinted toward the building. "Hey, *stop!*"

The woman slipped and tumbled to the ground. He holstered his gun, dropped the flashlight and grabbed her. Her head snapped around, her eyes wild with fear, her dark, spiky hair speckled with mud.

"Sam."

"Wesley," she heaved out as tears filled her eyes. "Wesley. Oh." The dam broke, and streaks slid down her face. "I thought you were..."

"Thought I was who?"

"Whoever I just saw in the woods. Someone..."

"Who?"

"I don't know! I was walking to my car, and I heard... I *felt...* I felt someone watching me. I turned, and someone was in the woods, staring right at me. He started coming toward me, and I screamed and took off."

"He?"

She nodded. "I think so. A big guy."

Wesley's eyes darted the landscape behind her. "Did you see where he went?"

"No. I screamed bloody murder and took off. Didn't look back."

He pulled her to her feet. "What were you doing going to your car?"

"I wanted to get the hell out of the hotel. Creeps me out. I couldn't find Lydia or Kaylee, and just wanted to leave. Or, sleep in my car until daylight. That place... it's evil."

"I saw Lydia a few minutes ago. She said they've been calling you and looking for you."

"I didn't get here 'till after eight. Checked into my room took a second to lay down, and I freaking fell asleep. I worked a double at the restaurant yesterday and worked late today. I was so exhausted. I woke up not long ago. My freakin' phone was on vibrate. I came downstairs, couldn't find them and just wanted to get the hell out."

"You didn't know the bridge collapsed?"

"It did?"

"Yeah, you wouldn't have gotten far." He handed her his flashlight. "We've got to get you back inside. Quickly."

"Lydia, *no.*"

With both hands, Gwen grabbed the trembling arms in front of her but Lydia yanked away. She was hysterical.

After seeing Kaylee's body, Gwen swiftly guided Lydia away from the balcony, but not before Lydia had gotten a quick glance of the scene.

The next few seconds had been a whirlwind. She'd heard the scream outside, then watched Wesley throw himself over the balcony in pursuit of something—someone —he'd seen below while she fought Lydia from running to her friend's body.

It had been five minutes of trying to calm her down. But trying to calm down a drunk woman was a losing battle.

"I'm not just going to stand here, feet away from Kaylee's body, waiting for Wesley! We have to get *help*, Gwen! Don't you see that?"

Wesley *was* the help, she thought but didn't say it. She also didn't want to remind Lydia that help wasn't going to come until the mountain reopened, more than likely after sunrise.

"I'm *going*!"

"*Where,* Lydia? Where the hell are you going to go?"

"Down to the lobby. That's where everyone is. Maybe someone... maybe we can get out of here."

Gwen shook her head. "We stay here, just like Wesley told us to do. He'll be back soon."

Lydia squinted her eyes in disgust and leaned forward, inches from Gwen's face. "Listen to yourself. Do you hear what you're saying? Do you know how many women have uttered those exact words? That Wesley would come back? Come back to them? You're just another notch on his fucking belt, Gwen. And you'll regret it." In a haste, she swooped down and took a flashlight from one end of the hall. "Mark my words, you'll regret the day you ever let Wesley Cross into your life. That is, unless your throat gets slashed first." With that final insult, Lydia spun on her heel and disappeared into the darkness, her flashlight bouncing on the walls reflecting the anger in her unsteady steps. The door to the stairwell popped open and slammed shut.

Then, silence.

Gwen stood, staring down the hallway, her heart pounding. Lydia's words were like a sledgehammer. She felt her chest squeezing and took a deep breath, another, and another.

The silence settled around her, suffocating. Haunting.

She turned, focusing on the single flashlight left in the hall. What if it went out? She clicked on her phone—47% battery. Worst case scenario, she'd have her cell phone light. She looked at the time—4:54 a.m. Dawn would begin to break in about thirty minutes.

Thirty minutes.

She glanced through the bar to the lump on the balcony, and her stomach rolled. For a second, she thought she might actually throw up. Her gaze shifted to the mountains in the distance, desperately willing Wesley to jump over the railing, tell her he caught the bastard, then take her away. Away from this Godforsaken hotel.

The silence became a heavy buzz in her ears, like a swarm of bees about to attack.

"*Shit,*" she whispered, her breath becoming shallower. She felt like she was on the brink of a full-blown panic attack.

"Okay, Gwen, you're okay... *you're okay.*" She'd officially resorted to talking to herself in an attempt to calm her nerves.

Her heart felt like a hammer beating her chest, collapsing her lungs. She wasn't okay. She had to get away from Kaylee's body. For a moment, she considered following Lydia downstairs, but she'd promised Wesley she wouldn't leave the floor.

He'd come back for her—despite what the drunk had said.

Gwen chewed on her lower lip and for the first time in her life, wished she had a gun. Maybe Wesley was right.

Maybe it was time to start carrying one, for situations just like this. Hell, she didn't even have mace. She shoved her hand in her purse, feeling around for anything she could use to protect herself when—*her room key!*

Her room!

Relief shot through her as she pulled it out, shone her light and read the number out loud.

"Four-twenty-eight." *Yes,* she would lock herself in her room until Wesley came back. With a surge of energy, she looped her purse around her shoulder and began frantically searching the numbers on the doors.

"Four-eighteen, Four-twenty..." Almost to the stairwell, she pushed into a jog. "Four-twenty-two, four, six, *eight.*"

Gwen grabbed the flashlight from the floor. Her hand trembled as she fumbled with the lock—an actual key, not a card.

"Come *on.*"

Finally, the door popped open. The faint smell of eucalyptus perfumed the air, pulling her back to hours earlier when she'd been trying on dresses. If she'd only known then what the night had in store for her. She quickly closed and locked the door, her hand instinctively reaching for the light switch, which didn't work of course.

"*Dammit.*"

Gwen lifted the flashlight and scanned the room. A king-sized, four-poster bed, a small loveseat, and an antique desk. A flat-screen hung from the wall, the only modern piece of furniture. Beside the bed was a small door which she guessed led to the bathroom, and beside that, a glass door flanked by windows overlooking a small balcony.

The sky was beginning to lighten.

Where was Wesley? Nerves tingled through her. Was he okay?

She clicked open a new text message.

Worried about you. Okay here. Lydia went back downstairs, couldn't stop her. I'm in my room, 428. Will wait for you here. Text back ASAP.

Gwen turned off the phone and stood for a moment, waiting for a response. A minute ticked by, her anxiety tripling with each second that passed without a response. She tossed her purse, heels, and phone on the bed and walked out onto the balcony, searching for Wesley below. The air smelled of wet earth. Water dripped off the over-filled gutters. A shiver caught her and she wrapped her arms around herself as she stepped to the edge.

Where was Wesley?

The clouds had moved on and the stars were beginning to dim with dawn.

Creak...

Gwen froze, clamped her mouth shut and strained to hear what sounded like footsteps behind her.

Someone was in her room.

It wasn't Wesley. Not only did her gut tell her that, but she knew he would've called out. And, he didn't have a key, anyway.

And then that unsettling thought gripped her. Who had a key?

Her fingers wrapped around the railing as her eyes darted the ground below, her brain desperately trying to devise a plan to get away. She was trapped, with nowhere to run.

Should she jump? Try to catch herself on the balcony below?

Panic ran like ants crawling over her skin.

She was in danger, every instinct in her body told her so.

Jump, Gwen, jump.

She gripped the railing, sucked in a breath and as she crouched to leap forward, a hand wrapped around her mouth.

everyone strict instructions to stay here. The lobby, or the bar. Is something wrong?"

"You do a headcount?"

"Yes, every hour."

"Do another now. I need to know who's missing. Bring the drunks in from the bar and do not let a single person leave this area, do you understand?"

Nodding, James clumsily pushed to a stance, his eyes wide with concern.

"I'll be back down in a minute."

As he jogged to the stairwell, he did a headcount of his own—James O'Connor and Cortez Vega playing chess; Lydia hyperventilating with Sam in the corner; Amelia Vega passed out on the staircase; the receptionist, Melanie, quietly reading a book behind the counter; the old man motionless and asleep—or dead, for all he knew—in an armchair by the window. His wife, knitting beside him. And Kaylee, dead as a doornail upstairs.

More than a few were missing. *Who?*

His mind raced.

The *hunters.* Bruce Jepsen and his mystery buddy, the guy in the pickup earlier.

Was that all that was missing?

Becks. Becks, the bartender, was also nowhere to be seen.

Wesley jogged across the lobby and pushed into the stairwell. He checked his phone as he raced up the steps—one new message from Gwen saying she was in her room.

Alone.

He burst onto the fourth floor and immediately noticed both flashlights were gone. An ice-cold chill ran up his back. He raised his gun and scanned as far as he could see through the darkness.

He jogged to room 428 and tried the knob—unlocked.

21

ITH SAM AT his side, Wesley jogged up the front steps. Every second that passed was a second away from Gwen. He pushed through the front doors and focused on the small crowd in the lobby gathered around a table topped with candles and empty wine bottles.

A gasp sounded beside him.

"*Sam!* Wesley!"

He turned, and his stomach dropped. "*Lydia.* What are you doing down here? I told you to stay with Gwen."

"I *couldn't,* Wesley, I couldn't be up there with... *oh, God, Sam!* Where the hell have you been?"

He pulled her attention back to him. "Where's Gwen, Lydia?"

"Up there. She stayed."

Shit. Fuck, fuck, fuck.

"Mr. Cross is everything okay?" Deep in the middle of a chess game with Cortez Vega, James frowned.

"Is everyone here in the lobby?" Wesley quickly asked.

Concern filled the bellman's eyes. "Yes, sir. Well, some are at the bar in the ballroom, but Melanie and I have given

"Gwen?" His voice boomed against the silence as he pushed open the door. His gaze landed on the flashlight that had once been at the end of the hall, now shining on a toppled-over chair on the balcony.

"Gwen!" He yelled as he ran outside but found no sign of her. There had been a struggle, and she was nowhere in sight. He spun on his heel and sprinted out of the room, noting her purse and phone on the bed. He took the stairwell and pulled out his phone.

Four rings passed. Finally, "Walker." The detective's voice was clipped, irritated.

"Dean, it's Wesley. Get your ass out of bed and get all available units to Half Moon. Send a fucking chopper if you have to. I've got a dead body, and Gwen is missing."

"Who? When?"

"Kaylee Rhodes is dead. I found her body less than an hour ago. But, Gwen is missing. He has her."

"Who has her?"

"Mikhail Lutrova. He broke out of prison, and he has her."

"That's impossible, Wesley."

"Why?"

"Because I'm staring down at Lutrova's dead body right now."

"What?"

"Shot. Jessica estimates he's been dead maybe two days."

Two days.

"Right after he murdered Leena."

"Yeah. If he did it."

Panic squeezed Wesley's chest. "Well, someone else is murdering people here at the Half Moon. I was lured here, Dean, by a bracelet on Leena's arm. It's got to be related. I don't have time to explain, just get everyone here."

"I will, as soon as I can. The bridge is out, but we'll find a way. I'll call the Sheriff now, get all available resources. Are you okay? Are you safe?"

"I am, *but Gwen's not*. Just get everyone here."

"I will. Hey, Jessica just told me that she got the DNA scan back on the blood around Leena's throat and Gwen's theory was right—there were two sets of DNA, human and animal. The eggs definitely came from a rotting animal carcass."

"What kind of animal?"

"She'll let us know ASAP."

Animal blood.

Wesley jumped onto the lobby floor landing and froze, hearing muffled voices from the basement level.

"I gotta go. Just get someone here, now." He slid his phone into his pocket, gripped his gun and jogged down the stairs. He peered out the stairwell door. The hallway was dark except for a candle flickering in Half Moon Jewelry. He raised his gun and descended down the hall. As he stepped inside the shop, he heard a shuffle behind him, and spun around.

"No! Don't shoot!" The candlelight reflected off Sally's thickly rimmed glasses, her eyes bugged with fear. Beside her, stood Sofia with a pair of rosary beads in her hands.

"Wesley," Sofia said quietly, with a hint of panic in her voice.

He lowered the gun. "Are you both okay?"

Sofia nodded. "Yes, yes. We've been down here together since the lights when out."

"Why aren't you in the lobby with everyone else?"

"Sofia wanted to stay with her store," Sally said. "So I stayed with her."

He looked them over. Their fear was palpable. "Have you seen anyone else down here?"

Sally nodded, her eyes filling with tears as Sofia twisted the beads in her hands. "Becks came down a little while ago."

Becks.

"And..." she lowered her voice to a whisper. "We just saw a girl being dragged down the hall."

His heart skipped. "Who?"

"Didn't get a good look at either of them." Sally sniffled. "But... the girl let out a squeak, and I swear... I swear it was Gwen."

"Who was dragging her?"

"We couldn't tell. It was so dark. We were just on our way up to the lobby to tell everyone and ask for help."

"When was this?" He asked quickly.

"Not even ten minutes ago."

"Where did they go?"

She pointed. "Down the hall, that way. Through the kitchen. We heard the back door open and close. I think she was taken outside."

"Go up to the lobby. Stay there."

"Okay... I'm sorry, Wesley. I'm sorry we didn't stop them."

"It's okay. *Go.*"

"Here, take this flashlight."

A second later, he burst into the kitchen. The air was cold and smelled of the freshly cooked dinners that were served before the electricity went out. He looked around, adrenaline pumping through him at breakneck speed. A large carving knife next to a chef's coat on the counter caught his eye. His gaze shifted to the unlatched door of the walk-in freezer. He raised his gun, silently jogged across the tiles, and paused. Silence.

As Wesley opened the heavy steel door, blood snaked beside his shoes, trailing from the crumpled body of Becks on the freezer floor, his head almost decapitated by the slice in his throat.

Jesus Christ.

Gwen.

Wesley sprinted out the back door. The putrid scent of rotting garbage assaulted him. An eerie, blue glow of dawn had dissolved the plague of darkness, but a dense fog was just beginning to form above the ground. He stood on a concrete slab lined with trash cans and dumpsters. A few chairs sat haphazardly next to the tree line, for smokers, he assumed. Flies buzzed overhead.

Flies.

Wesley watched the insects for a moment, noting their erratic pattern as they zipped in and out of the woods. He focused on a swarm, a black cloud, hovering just above a metal trash can nestled between two trees in the distance—the only can set aside. As he made his way over, the sour smell intensified. He swatted the flies, held his breath and peered into the can.

Thousands—*millions*—of maggots slithered in and out of skinned, rotting animal carcasses. He covered his nose with the back of his hand and looked closer. A brown and gray ringed tail, saturated with ooze and blood stuck out from the skinned carcasses.

A raccoon. The can was filled with skinned raccoons.

His eyes rounded.

Coon teeth... *the necklace.*

The cook.

22

*T*HE BACK DOOR creaked open behind him.

Wesley whipped around, gun raised.

"*No!* Wesley, it's Sofia." Hands raised, the jewelry store owner cautiously stepped outside.

Wesley lowered his gun but kept his finger on the trigger. "I told you to go upstairs."

Sofia slowly stepped across the concrete slab, her gaze drifting from the gun in his hand to his eyes, and Wesley had no doubt the woman hadn't come outside for some fresh air.

"Tell me," he said.

Her brow furrowed as she chewed on her lower lip. Her fingers twisted the rosary beads in her hand. "Wesley... I'm sorry..."

"*Tell me.*"

She took a deep breath, took a step closer. "I didn't tell you then... because, well, he's one of our own, you know... and we'd become friends, he and I. And you wouldn't tell me why you were asking about that pendant. You seemed so mad. I didn't want him to get in trouble."

"Tell me about Lawrence, the cook."

"He's the one who bought the cross pendant a few days ago. But I swear... that wasn't the person dragging Gwen down the hall."

"I thought you said you couldn't see the face."

"The shape of the body, the height, weight. I swear it wasn't Lawrence." She paused. "Where's Becks?"

"He's dead."

She gasped. Tears filled her eyes. "He must've seen whoever was dragging Gwen and confronted them...*Oh, God,* Wesley."

"Where's Lawrence now?"

"I don't know, I promise."

Just then—*snick.*

Wesley turned, aimed his gun into the woods. Over his shoulder, he whispered, "Go inside, Sofia. Now.*Go upstairs* and stay put until I get back or help arrives."

As the door clicked shut behind him, Wesley moved toward the tree line. The fog was thickening, raising from the earth like a blanket of ghosts, weaving in and out of the trees. He felt the moisture on his skin as he descended into the woods. He moved quickly, fluidly, through the thick underbrush, hyper-alert to any sound or movement around him.

His neck snapped toward a twig snapping just behind him. He squatted behind a rotted tree stump and froze. A rush of wind swept by, the rustling leaves playing tricks on him. He waited a few beats, then edged around the stump just as something moved away from a tree about fifteen feet ahead of him. He could barely make out the dark silhouette of a body through the fog, and he guessed it was a man. He set his jaw, narrowed his eyes and slipped through the thick underbrush like an animal tracking its prey.

The man stopped. Sensing him?

Wesley's finger slid over the trigger as he moved faster. The figure came into view, along with the gun in its hand.

"Drop your gun," Wesley snarled, his gun raised directly at the back of the man's head.

The man slowly raised his hands and surrendered his gun.

"Kick it and turn around."

The man turned. "Wesley Cross, I'm Thomas Grimes, FBI."

FBI?

"Show me your badge. Slowly."

Keeping one hand in the air, the man pulled out his wallet and kicked it to him. Wesley flipped it open and confirmed that the man was indeed, Thomas Grimes, with the Federal Bureau of Investigation.

"We're hunting the same man." Grimes said.

Wesley lowered his gun and stepped closer. "Lawrence Bennett."

Grimes nodded. "Since last night, or, early this morning, I should say. I've been in contact with Detective Dean Walker with BSPD, your buddy, apparently. I've been briefed on Leena Ross, your basement, and I also understand from Officer Willard you were asking about Mikhail Lutrova. I know everything."

"I know Mikhail's dead."

Thomas snorted. "Small town."

"Who killed him?"

"Don't know that, yet. Found shot dead in a barn on his grandmother's land... ten feet from a six-inch serrated knife with traces of dried blood."

Wesley's heart skipped a beat. "Leena's?"

"That's the assumption. Will know soon."

"What the hell does Lawrence have to do with all this?"

"Lawrence Bennett went to school in Missouri with Mikhail decades ago. They were buddies. His name is on the prison log several times over the last few years. Has a rap sheet, B&E, assault and several drug charges. Lutrova has also been sending encrypted emails to someone named Country Cutie. We traced the email to an IP address from a community computer out of the Berry Springs library. We're hunting Lawrence on the assumption he helped Lutrova break out of jail, and has helped him evade us for three damn days."

"Well, Grimes, I'm hoping you've got the track on him now because over the last twelve hours he's killed two people and kidnapped a third."

"Two?"

"Beckham, the bartender here, and Kaylee Rhodes."

Thomas's eyebrows tipped up. "Kaylee?" He shook his head. "I just visited her yesterday. Lawrence and Kaylee have been each other's booty calls for a few weeks. Guess he made his last call. Who's he have now?"

"Gwyneth Reece." A lump caught Wesley's throat as he said her name. Thomas noticed.

"A friend of yours, then."

"Yes. Enough chit-chat. Do you know where he is?"

"No, but there's a vehicle parked on the other side of the river."

"SUV?"

"Yep. Bullet holes in the back window. Sound familiar?"

Wesley's brows tipped up.

"We're assuming he parked there when he came to work so no one would ask questions. Then the bridge collapsed, so he's trapped."

"Let's go." They fell into step together. "You ran the plates?"

"Not yet, Bruce only just spotted it from a distance. He had to use one of the Half Moon fishing boats to cross the river to get to it. Should be there now, or close to."

"Bruce? Your partner?"

"Yes, Bruce Jepsen—

"You say Jepsen?"

"That's right."

"Cowboy hat, hung out solo in the ballroom last night? Chronic scowl on his face?"

"Yep. That's him." Thomas's breathing became labored as they hiked.

"Were you the guy in the red truck? Watching me last night?"

"Not watching only you."

Wesley hopped over a fallen tree and shook his head. "Something's not right. Doesn't add up. Mikhail killed Leena to send me a message. To lure me here, with the intention of killing me. It's revenge for getting him locked up. It's personal, Grimes. Why would Lawrence step in?"

"Because Lutrova died before the job was finished."

"No. It's Lutrova's fight, Lutrova's revenge. Doesn't add up."

"People have weird loyalties. I've been following him for three days now, and Lawrence was definitely spooked about something. Spooked about getting caught with Lutrova."

"Or, he made your tail. Knew he was being followed."

"Possible, I guess. *Stop.*"

Wesley froze and followed Thomas's gaze. Just ahead of them, a shadowy figure moved silently from tree to tree. He recognized the height, the weight—it was Lawrence. Alone.

He glanced at Thomas who gave a quick nod—*it's him.*

Wesley nodded toward the left and Thomas to his right. With guns raised, they split off to their respective sides and crept through the woods. The fog was rising, getting thicker by the minute.

Suddenly, Lawrence stopped, and Wesley zeroed in on the gun in his hand. He froze.

Lawrence raised the gun and slowly turned in the direction Thomas was supposed to be sneaking up on him.

Shit.

"Put your hands up!" Wesley shouted as he stepped out of the shadows.

Lawrence's body went rigid. He dropped the gun and raised his hands in the air. Thomas ran up from the side, pulling handcuffs from his belt.

Wesley lowered his gun and faced Lawrence as Thomas frisked him from the back, introducing himself as FBI.

Lawrence's long hair was frizzed from the humidity, loose strands falling over his pale face. Wesley glanced down at the raccoon necklace, then back at the snarling expression on his face.

"Where's Gwen?" Wesley demanded, keeping his gun on Lawrence while Thomas secured the cuffs.

"Who the fuck is Gwen?"

Wesley's eyes scanned from left to right behind the cook, his instincts screaming at him. This wasn't right. Something wasn't right.

"You're in a shitload of trouble, Lawrence." Thomas said. "Leena, Kaylee and Becks. The more you cooperate right now, the easier things will be for you. Trust me. Where's Gwyneth Reece?"

Lawrence's bloodshot eyes rounded, the slightest look of fear crossing his face. "Wait a second... you've got something wrong, man. I don't know a Gwen, and I don't know a Leena and I sure as hell didn't kill Becks. You've got the wrong person. And what about Kaylee?"

Thomas cut a glance at Wesley before saying, "Kaylee's dead."

"What?" Lawrence's face fell with shock.

Thomas paused, obviously sensing something wasn't right, just like Wesley was. Either Lawrence was one hell of a liar, or he wasn't the person they were looking for. And they were wasting time. "What brought you to Berry Springs two weeks ago, then?"

"My..." he stammered, his eyes wide now. "My old lady threw me out. Got a job here. Look, it ain't me."

Impatience shot like lightning through Wesley. Jaw clenched, he raised his gun directly between the cook's eyes. "Who has Gwen, Lawrence? I swear to God, I'll drop you right here."

Lawrence took a step back. "Okay. Alright. She does. I think, she does."

"Who's *she?*"

"Elise. Elise Barringer. The hotel maid."

"What the *fuck*?" Thomas said.

"I promise... I didn't know. We're friends, but she didn't say anything."

"You didn't know what?" Thomas asked.

"I didn't know what she was planning to do. To kill those people."

Wesley's head was spinning. "Talk *faster.*"

Lawrence continued, "She'd started acting really strange a few days ago. Asked me to buy her this ugly-ass pendant necklace from the jewelry store in the basement. And tonight, she was crazy. Really weird, man. Melanie even said she was trying to get keys to people's rooms. So, I began following her. I saw her dragging a brown-haired girl down the hall. So, I grabbed this gun from my truck and followed her."

"Your truck?" Thomas asked.

"Yeah. The blue Dodge, right out back."

"Where did she go?" Wesley's pulse roared in his ears.

"Toward the lake."

Gwen's chest heaved as she sprinted through the woods, her shallow breath raspy as she gasped for air. Tree limbs whipped past her face, jumping out of the fog without a moment's notice. She glanced over her shoulder. Had she lost her?

The maid.

Why didn't she see it? Why hadn't she even considered it?

She swiped the blood trickling down her neck from the blade Elise had held to her throat as she'd forced Gwen down the stairs and into the kitchen, where Becks had been searching for more liquor—talk about the wrong place at the wrong time. The moment he'd confronted Elise and distracted her, Gwen took her chance, elbowing the maid in the stomach and bolting out the back door.

She'd been running blindly for what seemed like ten minutes. She didn't know where she was, or where Wes was, just that she needed to get as far away from the evil hotel as possible.

Her toe clipped a rock and she stumbled, catching herself on a tree.

She swallowed deeply between breaths, her mouth so dry it felt like cotton. She sucked in a breath, held, and listened as the waves of fog swayed around her. In the distance, she heard the faint sound of water.

The lake.

The picture of fishing boats from the brochure flashed in her head. After taking one last glance over her shoulder, she maneuvered through the woods until her feet hit the sandy shore. Just ahead, the dock, with two fishing boats. She sprinted across the shore, the sand kicking up from her feet.

Get the hell out of here. Now.

The dock creaked as she jumped onto it. She found the boat keys in an old, wooden box mounted to a utility closet. One tumbled from her trembling hand, settling between two slats. She grabbed the other, darted to the closest boat and began frantically untying it from the dock.

Her heart raced.

Come on, come on.

And just as she yanked the rope from the hitch, pain exploded through her skull.

Wesley spun on his heel and took off through the woods, the fog, the thickest he'd ever seen, completely engulfed him as he neared the riverbank. He squinted, barely able to make out the rickety dock just ahead of him.

Hang on, Gwen, was all he'd thought as he leapt onto the dock. A piece-of-shit fishing boat swayed in the water, next to two empty slips. His gaze shifted to a pair of keys lying in the middle of the dock. He picked them up and looked around. Gwen had been there, very recently. He knew it in his gut. He untied the only remaining boat, jumped in and pushed away from the dock.

The air was cool, the fog so heavy around him it felt like a wet blanket coating his skin. He took off through the water, the little boat topping out at fifteen miles an hour. Branches, fallen logs, and trash littered the river from the storm. If he hit a decent sized log, it was a good chance the shit-boat would tip. But that was the least of his concerns.

How would he see Elise's boat through the fog?

He shook his head.

The maid. *What the fuck?* He tried to picture her in his head but the image was fuzzy. He'd only seen her once, from across the room, but she definitely *wasn't* in the lobby when he'd dropped off Sam. But how the hell did she tie into all this? And, who had killed Mikhail? Two huge pieces of the puzzle were still missing.

He had to get to Gwen—every second that passed was potentially her last. He'd told her she'd be safe, safe with him. He couldn't let her down. He couldn't lose her. He ground his teeth so hard pain shot through his head.

Goddammit Wes, why did you leave her?

His chest rose and fell with adrenaline.

I'm coming, Gwen. I'm coming.

Just then, he heard the echo of voices bounce off the bank—*shouts*. He veered toward the noise, lost in a gray cloud of fog.

"...*hands up!*" His heart stopped at the sound of her voice.

Bobbi. His sister. His *sister?!*

Wesley frantically scanned the fog, locking on a dark object in the middle of the river.

What the fuck was his sister doing out there?

The object began to take shape as he drew closer. Elise, with her wild, black hair blowing in the wind, stood behind Gwen with her arm wrapped around her neck, and he had no doubt a knife was pressed to Gwen's neck. And just beyond that, his sister stood in his ski boat, with a gun pointed at both women. All his years running special ops for the Marines couldn't prepare him for this moment.

Did Bobbi see him coming up from behind? Could she, through the fog? The last thing he needed was for his sister to go all Annie Oakley on everyone, and they'd all be toast. He cut the engine and grabbed an oar, and began creeping up on Elise's boat.

"Drop the knife!" His sister shouted.

"Not until I see Wesley Cross!"

Wesley paddled faster until he was less than fifteen feet from the boat. He dropped the oar and pulled out his gun. His hand trembled as he raised it.

Suddenly, he heard Gwen yelp and a fresh rush of adrenaline shot like lightning through him. Gwen didn't have long.

"What do you want with my brother?"

The buzz in his ears faded, the shouts, the sound of the water lapping against the boat, it all faded away as he aimed the gun and slid his finger around the trigger.

Gwen screamed.

Pop!

Elise's body crumbled as Gwen dove into the water. Wesley tossed his gun and dove in, the cold water knocking the breath out of his lungs as he swam like a bullet through the water.

"Wesley!" Gwen cried out through the fog.

He propelled his body toward her voice until finally, he wrapped his arms around her.

"Are you okay?" He frantically wiped the strings of hair from her face, looking her over.

"Yes." She coughed and spat water. "Yes, I'm okay."

He zeroed in on the knot on the side of her head and the

thin trickle of blood running down her neck, spreading into the dark water.

"I'm okay, Wes. The knife barely pierced me. *Oh, my God, Wes.*"

"Wes! Are you okay?"

He looked past Gwen to see Bobbi yelling from the tip of the boat, then shifted his gaze to the fishing boat swaying in the water.

"You're sure you're okay?" He asked again.

Gwen nodded, her teeth chattering.

He kissed her, feeling the warmth and comfort from her mouth. She was okay, and his sister was okay.

"I've got to get you to my sister's boat."

"Your *sister?*"

"Explain later. Come on..."

He guided Gwen to the ski boat. Bobbi leaned over, grabbed for Gwen.

"On three... one, two, three."

Wesley hoisted Gwen up and pinned his sister. "Bobbi, what the *fuck* are you doing here?"

Bobbi wiped the sweat from her brow. "You said you were going to come by last night but never showed. Then, I heard about Mikhail escaping jail, and tried to call but didn't get through. *Then* I heard that the bridge had collapsed and you were trapped! So I went and got your damn boat, came up the river and stumbled on this fucking hot mess." She nodded toward Elise's fishing boat.

"I told you to stay out of this." He nodded toward Gwen. "Wrap her up, will ya? This is Gwen."

Bobbi's eyebrows tipped up, then she said, "Okay. Be careful. You still got your gun?"

"No."

She handed him hers. "I'm right here."

"Thanks, Sis." He smiled, then dove under and swam to the fishing boat.

Wesley breached and treaded water for a moment until a low moan drifted into the air. He gripped the side and looked over. A river of red pooled in the bottom, the blood trickling from the bullet wound in the maid's leg—exactly where he'd aimed. She writhed in pain, rocking back and forth until her eyes opened and locked on his.

And his blood froze as he stared into the chilling, ice-blue eyes.

Ice-blue.

23

Five hours later...

WESLEY CROSSED HIS arms over his chest as he stared into the little window of interview room two.

"You're looking at Inna Lutrova, Mikhail's mother." Sliding his phone into his pocket, Dean walked up behind him.

"His *fucking* mother. Unbelievable. I knew it the moment I saw those eyes."

"Chilling, huh? Let's head to my office," Dean nodded toward the end of the hall.

"How's her leg?"

"Cleaned and stitched-up. Didn't even need surgery. She's fine. You get your truck?"

"No, Bobbi took me by the house to change into some dry clothes before coming here. I got the farm truck."

They stepped into the detective's closet-sized office. Dean closed the door, tossed a stack of papers on his desk and glanced at the red blinking light on his voicemail. He blew out a breath.

Based on the dark circles and bags under the detective's eyes, Wesley knew he hadn't gotten a lick of sleep in the last twenty-four hours, or returned any calls, apparently.

"Yep, she's his damn mother," Dean said. "Been using the name and identity of Elise Barringer for the last twenty-something years."

"Why?"

"Finally had enough of her husband, Mikhail's stepdad, beating the shit out of her. Packed a bag and skipped town one night. Went down to Mexico, created a new life for herself, then came back here as Elise. Dyed her hair, lost a lot of weight. Got a job at the Half Moon last year."

"Couldn't hide those eyes, though."

Dean frowned. "Like staring into pure evil."

"She didn't take Mikhail when she left?"

"No. He went into protective services. Got shuffled through the system." He paused. "You know he was abused, too, right? It was pretty bad."

Wesley nodded. "Where's the stepdad now?"

"Dead. Died in prison decades ago. Heart attack."

"Nice."

"Yeah. Anyway, Inna has been in communication with Mikhail since he was put away... since *you* put him away. She's Country Cutie, the person he'd been emailing, the person the FBI thought was Lawrence. She picked him up when he busted out of prison, brought him down here. They both hid out in his grandmother's barn, out on her land. Granny's been dead eleven years. Mikhail inherited the land. That's where we found him." He took a deep breath. "Killing Leena was the start of the plan he'd spent five years conjuring up in his head, with his mom's help, of course. Revenge for you getting him locked up."

"But he died before he could finish the job. Who killed him?"

Dean's gaze pinned him from across the room. "You did."

"What?" Wesley's hands dropped to his side.

"Mikhail had a bullet wound right under his right shoulder, barely puncturing the top of his lung. His black SUV, which Inna has been driving since, has two bullet holes through the back glass and blood all over the seat."

Wesley's eyes rounded.

"Yep. You barely missed his head the night you chased him off your property. According to Jess, he lived for hours before dying in the barn, in his mother's arms. Bled out. Poetic ending if you ask me."

"And Inna took up his sword."

"Exactly. And with plenty of rage considering you'd just killed her son. She'd been using Lawrence, Mikhail's childhood friend, as a pawn. Maybe hoping to pin everything on him, we guess. She stole his knife from the kitchen and gave it to Mikhail to use on Leena. Jessica confirmed it was raccoon blood on Leena's neck."

"That's where the eggs came from. Gwen was right."

"Yep. So we've got the murder weapon, and his bloody SUV that you shot puts him on the scene. Case closed."

"For Leena. What about Kaylee and Becks?"

"After interviewing Lawrence, we've put together that Kaylee had gone to the fourth-floor bar to confront him about everything, and Inna stepped in. Took care of that potential crack in her plans. And Becks confronted her when she had Gwen, got him killed. Woman was blinded by rage." A pair of knuckles rapped at the door. Dean glanced through the window at the suit on the other side. "I gotta go. Are they done with you?"

"Think so. Been through four hours of interviews." He glanced at the clock. "And, actually, I gotta run, too." He paused. "Thanks, Dean."

Dean smiled. "We're even, then."

Wesley stepped into the hall, almost running into Bobbi and Jessica.

"Hey!" Bobbi's face lit the moment she saw him.

He smiled. "How's it feel to be the town hero?"

"Yeah, right. I'll feel a lot better once they let me out of this station. I've got a six-pack and king-sized bed with my name on it."

"You've earned it." He shifted his attention to Jessica. "How you doing?"

"Just wading my way through this damn circus." She reached into her pocket and slid a small bag into his hand. "That favor you asked me; it's clean. Not that it really matters now, anyway." Her eyes filled with sadness. "Thought you might want to hang onto it."

He squeezed the bracelet in his hand and slid it into his pocket. "Thank you."

Jessica glanced at her watch. "Well, boys and girls, I'm meeting with the suits in five. Then, gathering up the dead bodies and heading to work. Wish me luck."

"Good luck. And, Jess, thanks again."

After a wink, the medical examiner disappeared down the hallway. Wesley looked at his watch. "Hey, I've got something to do real quick. Find me before you head out, okay?"

"Will do."

He looked down at his sister, and his heart swelled. "You were really brave, Sister."

She smiled. "Nobody fucks with the Crosses."

"That's right. Nobody fucks with the Crosses." He kissed her forehead. "Don't leave without finding me." As he walked down the hallway, she called out after him. "Wes?"

He stopped, turned. "Yeah?"

"Give her a chance, Wes." She smiled. "I like her."

Wesley dipped his chin, turned and jogged down the hall, past the crowded bullpen and men in suits. Jessica was right, the police station was a circus. The moment he pushed out the doors, a cool breeze carrying the fresh scent of fall swept past him. The fog had lifted. The sky was a stunning sapphire blue, the leaves had hit their prime, glowing bright colors of orange and red in the sunlight. It was a beautiful morning, made all the more perfect by the stunning brunette leaning against his truck. Their eyes met, and a smile spread over his face.

He took a deep breath as he walked down the steps, the tension instantly releasing from his shoulders.

Gwyneth Reece was safe.

"Hey, there," Gwen said as a strand of hair swept across her face.

He got the butterflies, and without saying a word, grabbed her face and kissed her.

"Wow," Gwen whispered as he pulled away. "I like your hellos."

He ran his fingers through her hair, soaking in the silky feeling of each strand, the warmth of her skin, the curves of her face. "Thanks for coming by."

"I just saw your sister."

"You've made quite an impression on her."

"Same goes. You both saved my life..." She frowned and looked down. "Thank you isn't enough."

"You've given her a hell of a story and bragging rights for years. That's enough, trust me. She'll milk this 'till the day she dies. And you've thanked me enough, too, so enough of that."

She stared at him for a moment, and a dozen more butterflies entered his stomach.

"Anything new?" She asked.

"Inna's in federal custody now. She'll be locked up for the rest of her life. Gwen, you were right about everything. She'd taken Lawrence's knife that he used to skin his coons and gave it to Mikhail to kill Leena. You were right."

She nodded, glanced down as the weight of the morning filled her face.

He tipped up her chin. "You're a hell of a detective, you know that?"

"Entomologist."

"In your head, same thing."

She smiled. "Thank you for keeping me updated through the morning."

After Gwen had given her statement at the scene, they let her go back to her room to clean up while Wesley had been told to head to the station. The truth was, he'd texted and called her more times than he could count over the last five hours because he needed to hear her voice, be close to her somehow. He needed her comfort.

She checked her watch. "I've got to go."

"Flight at two, right?"

"Right." She glanced away.

"You know, I was thinking..."

"Yeah?"

"You really should take that trip to Hawaii. You deserve it."

She laughed. "God, that sounds like heaven right about now."

"With me."

Her eyebrows slowly lifted.

"Let's go. You and me."

"To *Hawaii*?"

"Why not?" He trailed a finger down her cheek, kissed her again.

"You keep kissing me like that, I'll do whatever you say."

He kissed her again.

"When?" She grinned.

"Next week."

"*Next week?*" She laughed, shook her head. "I can't just... I'll have to look at my—

"Clear it. Let's do it."

She stared at him with a mix of disbelief and excitement.

"Gwen, I don't just want to say goodbye. I don't want this to be it."

Tears filled her eyes. "Me either, Wes."

He swept her off her feet. "I'm crazy about you, Gwen. I am." He smelled her hair, that indescribable scent of *her,* and couldn't fight the smile that crossed his lips. It felt *right. She* felt right. "We'll go to the most romantic place on earth and just take it from there. And if there's a wedding dress involved, so be it."

She laughed and kissed his cheek. "If we ever leave the room."

∼

SNEAK PEEK

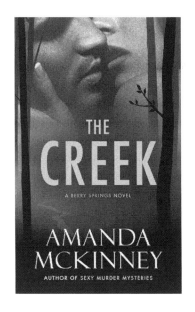

THE CREEK

When DNA evidence links Lieutenant Quinn Colson's brother to the scene of a grisly murder, Quinn realizes

he'll do anything to keep his brother from returning to prison, even if it costs him his job... and the woman who's stolen his heart.

Shooting range owner by day, yoga instructor by night, Bobbi Cross is as ironic as her two businesses—she's an independent, tough-as-nails woman, except when she's meditating away the discontentment she feels inside. But no amount of Zen can help her when she finds her business partner bludgeoned to death in a burning house. The scene is something straight out of a horror movie, excluding the smothering hot Police Lieutenant who saves her from the flames.

Quinn Colson accepted a position at the police department in the small, southern town of Berry Springs for one reason —to keep an eye on his little brother, newly released from prison. He couldn't care less that the locals eye him like the plague, until he meets a green-eyed stunner at the scene of his first big case. Bobbi Cross is nothing like anyone he's ever met, and when they team up to solve her friend's murder, it becomes evident that no woman in town is safe from the ruthless killer, including Bobbi.

With a mountain of evidence that doesn't appear to link together, the case is as confusing as his growing feelings for the town's sweetheart... until a DNA test connects his brother to the scene of the crime. In an instant, Quinn's world is turned upside down, and he realizes he'll do anything to keep his brother from returning to prison, even if it costs him his job... and the woman who's stolen his heart.

THE CREEK is a standalone romantic suspense novel.

Grab your copy of the THE CREEK today!

ABOUT THE AUTHOR

Amanda McKinney is the bestselling and multi-award-winning author of more than twenty romantic suspense and mystery novels. Her book, Rattlesnake Road, was named one of *POPSUGAR's 12 Best Romance Books,* and was featured on the *Today Show.* The fifth book in her Steele Shadows series was recently nominated for the prestigious *Daphne du Maurier Award for Excellence in Mystery/Suspense.* Amanda's books have received over fifteen literary awards and nominations.

Text **AMANDABOOKS to 66866** to sign up for Amanda's

Newsletter and get the latest on new releases, promos, and freebies!

www.amandamckinneyauthor.com

If you enjoyed The Fog, please write a review!